MINUTES LATER

DANIEL HURST

www.danielhurstbooks.com

This is a work of fiction. Names, characters, businesses, places, events, locales, and incidents are either the products of the author's imagination or used in a fictitious manner. Any resemblance to actual persons, living or dead, or actual events is entirely coincidental.

20 MINUTES LATER

First edition. April 3, 2020.

Written by Daniel Hurst

June in London, England

Monday morning

Events take place between 08:28 - 08:48

20 Minutes after the Tube

Jelena

08:28

Somewhere in Central London

Jelena Markovic heard the sirens first. It was impossible not to. They were deafening.

She could also hear voices. Two men. Both close to her.

It sounded like one of the men was just inches from her face, and she felt that familiar wave of panic rising up from her stomach once more.

It was happening to her again.

She opened her eyes and without thinking, began to hit out at whoever was nearby. The nearest man took a fist to the side of the head and recoiled in shock. The second man did his best to control the flailing arms, but he too fell victim to the spontaneous anger coming from the frightened woman.

With the men forced into a momentary retreat, Jelena tried to sit up and escape from the position she was in. But something was holding her down.

She looked at her waist and saw a thick black strap stretched across it.

She was tied to the bed.

Oh god, it was happening again.

She pulled at the strap, expecting to have little success but, to her surprise, it came away easily. They hadn't restrained her as forcefully as they usually did. Maybe now was her chance to get away. She pulled the strap loose from her torso and sat up fully on the bed, but before she had the chance to swing her legs over the side she saw one of the men coming back for her, his arms outstretched, reaching for the strap she had just removed.

Quick as a flash, Jelena turned the strap into a weapon and whipped it across the man's face, hearing it slap against his pasty white cheeks. The man was stunned into silence and held his hand to his face as he recoiled in shock.

You don't like it when I fight back, do you? she thought to herself as she sneered at him and gripped the strap tightly, ready to use it again if necessary. That's when she noticed the second man coming towards her again, and she readied herself and her weapon for the next attack.

But suddenly the strap was taken from her by an unseen force, and another hand gripped her skinny wrist tightly. She was just about to scream and spit in the direction of her third captor when he spoke.

"Jelena, it's okay. These men are trying to help you."

She didn't recognise the voice, but there was something in it that sounded soothing. The words had been spoken in English, but they were delivered with a thick Eastern European accent, and they didn't contain any of the venom that she had become so accustomed to recently. She felt the grip on her fragile wrist loosen and turned to see who had spoken to her. As soon as she saw who it was, a cascade of memories washed over her.

The man's face was pale. His facial hair was thick and slightly bushy, although his mop of black hair was more presentable. And his eyes were a piercing blue, though they were surrounded by evidence of fatigue. He was fairly unremarkable to look at, but at that moment, he was the best thing she could have seen. Because suddenly she remembered what had happened.

She had been rescued by this man - this man from her hometown, who had once been a boy at her school in Belgrade.

Bogdan.

His face softened, and his beard bristled as his mouth stretched into a warm, caring smile.

"It's okay. We're going to the hospital," he said as he tried to guide Jelena back down onto her pillow.

Jelena saw the two men moving closer to her again in her peripheral vision and turned to see them but only now, in her more relaxed state, did she properly take note of who they were. Or more importantly, who they weren't.

Now that she had calmed down, it was clear that these weren't the two men who had seized her off the lorry from Belgrade and thrown her into a life of misery. These weren't the two men who had kept her locked away like a prisoner for so many months. And these weren't the two men who had forced her into sex with strangers in a small, windowless room in a godforsaken part of London. They were just two paramedics, and they were simply trying to help her.

Having realised with considerable relief that the perceived danger was not real, she took the time to look at her surroundings. It was clear now that she wasn't back in that hellhole of a room where she had spent so many days and nights being abused and betrayed. She was in the back of an ambulance. Now the sirens made sense. Bogdan was right. She was on her way to the hospital.

She was suddenly aware of how weak she felt, but before she allowed her body to sink back into the soft surface it was stationed on, she glanced back at Bogdan for confirmation that everything was really what it seemed. His warm smile and caring eyes gave her the reassurance she was seeking and, gratefully, she gave herself permission to lie back down on the bed. The paramedics were clearly relieved about this and positioned themselves beside her as she rested her head on the thin pillow behind her.

As she watched the two men in uniform go about their work, both of them now sporting sizeable evidence of her panicked attack a few moments ago, she did her best to try and recall the moments that had led to her being here. The last thing she could remember was being in Bogdan's arms on the train platform, hugging him tightly and crying into his broad shoulders. She had just fled from the man from whom she had spent months trying to escape, and her body had been overrun with an array of vivid emotions. Relief, excitement, anger, remorse. She had experienced the full spectrum as she had leant into Bogdan's chest and sobbed her heart out.

But then it had gone dark.

She suspected she had fainted, but couldn't be sure, although it would explain the gap in her memory between the platform and this speeding ambulance. With the amount of adrenaline running through her at the time, she could hardly be blamed for losing consciousness. The fact that she seemed to be in safe hands now was a relief. But still, she couldn't relax, despite Bogdan's continued efforts to soothe her. She wanted to speak, to ask him what had happened, how he had found her and, most of all, where her captor was.

Had he been caught? Was he in the back of a police car now? Was he being questioned? And what about the other one? Had he been caught too? Or were they both still out there and were they going to come for her again?

She had so many questions, but getting the answers to them would prove difficult for her. *After all, communicating her queries without a tongue would be impossible.*

The agonising operation that had removed it was her punishment for a previous escape attempt, but the consequences were far-reaching. The ordeal may have ended, but her suffering never would. She would never speak again. Therefore, she needed to articulate her questions in a different way. Maybe if she could get a pen and write them down, she could get some answers.

She signalled her intention to Bogdan by moving her frail hand across the air in front of him as if forming words. He understood immediately but shook his head.

"You need to rest," he told her in their native language.

Jelena shook her head and made the same signal again. The paramedics paused in their work for a moment and watched the interaction, not sure what Jelena was asking for and definitely not sure what Bogdan's responses translated as.

Jelena frantically continued performing the international sign for writing, and this time the paramedics seemed to understand. They also understood Bogdan's response because he had stopped speaking and was simply shaking his head.

Jelena hit the bed with both fists, feeling the frustration in every pore of her body. *This is what it's going to be like forever,* she thought. *I'll never have a normal conversation again.*

She tried to fight it, but it was impossible to stop the tears rolling down her cheeks. She turned her face away from the men in an attempt to disguise her state of mind, but it was too late. They had seen. If Jelena had been looking at Bogdan, she would have noticed that tears had formed in his eyes too. Instead, she just stared at the wall of the ambulance beside her and fought to control her emotions.

After around twenty seconds, she felt a gentle hand on her shoulder. Instinctively she flinched, but then she realised it was just Bogdan and he was offering her something.

It was a pen and a folded piece of paper. He smiled at her and held it closer for her to take.

Jelena wiped the tears from her eyes and took the tools that would now perform the role of her voice. She took a deep breath and started writing, but it wasn't easy using her leg as a writing surface, and the pen moved sloppily across the paper.

She looked around for something better to support her and quickly decided to use the ambulance wall. This too had its difficulties, with every turn on the route or bump in the road causing the paper to move and the pen to slide across it unintentionally. But finally, Jelena was able to finish writing her first question. She lowered the pen and held the paper out to Bogdan.

He took it and tried to decipher the scrawl written across it. The motion of the ambulance, combined with the weakness of Jelena's wrists, caused by months of malnutrition and abuse, meant that her writing was far from clear. To the two paramedics watching on, it would have been downright undecipherable, even if it had been written in English as opposed to Serbian. But Bogdan persevered, with Jelena waiting patiently at his side, and eventually, he understood her first question, which was: 'Why can't I remember how I got here?'

"You fainted. Right after you got to me," he told her.

Jelena nodded then snatched the paper back, eager to continue this little game of theirs. She scribbled something new then thrust it back into Bogdan's large, warm hands.

He read it and smiled a little, and Jelena noticed the glint in both eyes that suggested he had been crying a little too since they had been in this ambulance.

"I saw you on the escalator and followed you down to the platform. It was just chance," he said, in response to her questioning how he had been able to help her.

Now he said it, Jelena vaguely remembered something happening on the escalator. There had been shouting. She had experienced a strong feeling of hope. Then she had been pulled away by her captor and dragged onto the nearest train.

Jelena stared at Bogdan and studied his face again. Yes, she could recall seeing him on the escalator. Just like she could recall his younger face looking at her across the playground during one of their lunch breaks at school.

While the beard and the lines on his forehead gave away his current age, which she assumed must be twenty-eight, the same as hers, his eyes still had that softness and kindness in them that they had held as a child. At that moment, despite everything, she wanted to ask him what he had been doing in the time that had passed since school. She wanted to know what had brought him to London. She wanted to know why he cared about her so much. But there was one far more pressing question that she needed to address first. The answer would be the difference between her being able to relax enough for the paramedics to do their work and her potentially fainting for a second time today.

She felt the ambulance turning a corner and waited for the vehicle to correct itself before she began writing again. When she finished, she stared at the paper in her hand. The other questions had filled in the gaps in her memory since her rescue. But this one was more powerful. It could give her peace of mind, which was something she hadn't had for months. She hoped with every fibre of her exhausted, malnourished body that she would finally get the serenity that she so desperately craved.

Jelena handed the piece of paper to Bogdan and held her breath as he read her query. She tried to read his face for a reaction before he spoke, but he was stone-faced. He was nervous about this answer and Jelena wasn't sure if that was a good or bad sign.

All she wanted to know was if they had caught the man who had been with her on the tube. If they had, he was presumably now in custody and hopefully his accomplice was too. The authorities would also be able to search the flat where they had kept her for clues and, most likely, their findings would be enough to bring down their whole sex-trafficking operation. The address of the other flat, where she had been taken to meet the depraved men who paid to rape, would either be discovered or confessed and hopefully they would be able to trace all the customers who had been a part of this sordid, illegal and despicable business. Best of all, it would mean no other women would be used like Jelena had, and families could be reunited while those who tore them apart would pay for their crimes. But the longer Bogdan failed to give her the answer, the less likely this outcome seemed to be.

She reached out and grabbed his wrist. As he looked into her eyes, he didn't need speech to know what she was saying.

Tell me.

Jelena held her breath as Bogdan answered.

"I'm sorry," he finally said. *"He got away."*

Vukasin

08:29

Turner Crescent, Brockmore Estate,

North London

Vukasin Dordevic felt like he was having a heart attack, so he leant against the brick wall of the building he was standing beside and sucked in as much oxygen as he could. His decision to run here from the tube station was a necessary one, but that didn't mean it was a wise one. Not for someone in his physical condition. He hadn't run like this in years, but if he wasn't quick then it would be the last time that he would be able to run as a free man.

He pushed himself away from the wall and forced himself to keep going. His sizeable stomach wobbled above the line of his belt, and his legs strained against the jeans that were encasing them. To a casual observer, he must have looked ridiculous. He was an overweight man attempting to sprint while dressed in a large shirt, baggy jeans and heavy boots. But if that casual observer had known what he was running from, then they would have understood exactly why he was straining every sinew to get to his destination quicker.

Vukasin turned the corner of the street, and finally, the end was in sight. He could see the door that led to the small flat that he and his colleague Laslo rented. The flat in which they had kept the Serbian woman who had been making them a fortune for the past four months. Laslo would be in there, probably eating and making a mess of the place. But Jelena would not be there.

Because she was gone.

How the hell could I have let this happen? Vukasin screamed internally to himself as he continued his slog back to the flat. But he knew the answer even if he didn't want to admit it.

The decision to start transporting Jelena on the Underground after their van had broken down was, with hindsight, a foolish one. Cutting off her tongue after her previous escape attempt had successfully broken her will to try anything again, but they had failed to account for somebody else setting her free.

Vukasin knew that the man on the escalator had been the reason he had lost his grip on Jelena. *But who was he?* Somehow, he had known Jelena and had called to her. His voice had reinvigorated her and given her the strength and courage to escape. *But what were the odds of somebody recognising Jelena here, miles from Serbia, in a train station tunnel deep below London?*

Yet as crazy as it seemed it had happened and now it was only a matter of time until Jelena brought the police to this flat to arrest him and Laslo. He had to get back and warn his friend so they could clear the flat of any evidence. They needed to get the hell out of the country before the authorities issued their photos to every possible port of escape, trapping them and ensuring that it was only a matter of time until they were behind bars.

The clock was ticking.

Finally, Vukasin reached the door to the flat and fumbled for the key in his jeans pocket. But in his haste, he dropped it, and it clattered across the concrete before coming to a stop only inches away from a sewage grid. If the key had gone down there, then he might as well have given up. But it was retrievable, and he could only hope the rest of his situation would be too.

He pushed the key into the lock and turned it hard, almost snapping it off its keyring in his desperation, before pushing open the door and bounding up the stairs.

"LASLO!" he shouted at the top of his voice as he climbed the staircase and reached the next door. Of course, this one was also locked, an extra security measure they had put in place when they had taken the flat, knowing full well they intended to use it to house a kidnapped woman. But now it was just another obstacle pushing him closer towards that prison cell.

Vukasin reached into his pocket for the second key. He knew that this one had already worked itself free from the loose keyring that had connected it to the first one, and he was kicking himself for not taking the time to fix it before now.

His fingers fumbled desperately inside his jeans pocket, but it was no good. Time was running out, so he gave up and hammered on the door as hard as he could.

"LASLO! OPEN THIS FUCKING DOOR!" he screamed in Serbian to the man inside.

He heard a chair scraping and a bottle hit the floor, smashing into a million pieces and causing an explosion of ugly swear words.

That lazy bastard has already started drinking, Vukasin thought as he heard another bottle topple over.

"WHERE'S YOUR FUCKING KEY?" came the cry from the other side and Vukasin could feel his grip on time beginning to lose its strength.

Before long, this door would be kicked in by police officers, and they had to be gone before that happened or they would be spending the rest of their lives in prison cells.

"OPEN THE DOOR YOU STUPID BASTARD" Vukasin screamed, not caring if the neighbours either side of their flat could hear what was going on.

The neighbours would undoubtedly be questioned by the police at some point, and while they might be able to back up Jelena's description of them, they wouldn't have much else to say. He and Laslo had deliberately kept a low profile since moving in. They had been careful not to raise any suspicions during their stay and had done a good job of it too. Soundproofing Jelena's room had been easier than expected, and Vukasin suspected some of the neighbours may not have even been aware that there had been a woman living here with them at all. They had blended into the background of London life extremely well. Until today. Soon everybody in this city would be looking for them and so the time for being discreet was over.

Vukasin pounded on the door again and was just beginning to fancy his chances of knocking it off its hinges when he heard the handle click.

The moment of silence that the two men shared when the door finally opened didn't last long.

"What the hell are you doing back here?" Laslo demanded to know. But then he noticed that Vukasin was alone and realised that the answer would not be a good one.

Vukasin pushed past him and stormed through the kitchen, ignoring the mess of empty food packets and broken beer bottles and heading for the corridor at the back.

"Where the fuck is she?" Laslo called after him, but Vukasin said nothing, instead just going straight to the bedroom he had taken for himself when they first moved in.

His room was at the end of the corridor closest to the kitchen and bathroom, Laslo's was at the far end of the corridor, and Jelena had been kept in the middle one. It had been a tactical choice to put her there, as it meant she wasn't able to bang on the walls and raise the alarm with the neighbours on the other side. The more Vukasin thought about it, the more it seemed crazy that he had ever been confident enough to take her on the train. They had gone to so much effort to kidnap her, keep her locked away and boost their profits from prostituting her, yet it had all been undone by one stupid decision.

If only the damn van hadn't broken down, Vukasin thought to himself as he grabbed his duffel bag and threw his possessions untidily inside it.

He was just about to reach for the Rolex that he had treated himself to a fortnight ago and had forgotten to wear this morning when a strong hand grabbed his arm and spun him around.

It was Laslo, and he wanted answers.

"Tell me what happened," he said, his eyes moving to the hastily packed duffel bag on the bed behind his sweating friend. The sight of Vukasin packing was all the information he really needed to know, but he still wanted more.

"Some guy at the station. He fucking knew her. She got away from me," Vukasin explained, the shaking in his voice contrasting with the dominant energy he so often expressed around his partner in crime.

"What do you mean he knew her? What guy?" Laslo demanded, just as confused about the whole situation as the man who had actually witnessed it.

"It doesn't matter. She got away. And the police will be here any minute so get your shit and let's get the fuck out of here."

Vukasin turned back to his bed and continued packing. But Laslo remained still behind him, seemingly frozen to the spot.

"LASLO!" Vukasin barked when he noticed the inefficient man still standing in his doorway. The volume of his voice was enough to send Laslo scarpering down the corridor towards his own room.

Vukasin finished packing and thought about trying to wipe the room for prints but decided it was futile. They would be all over the flat, and there was no way he would be able to eradicate them all. Besides, he already had a criminal record back in Serbia. As soon as the police were able to pull his image from the numerous CCTV cameras in the Underground and put it into their system, they would soon have his name and would issue a warrant for his arrest. There was no stopping that now. All he could do was try to delay his capture for as long as possible.

He grabbed his bag and left his room, passing through the corridor and back into the kitchen.

"WE LEAVE NOW!" he called out to Laslo, who was now on the other side of the flat, packing his own belongings and presumably doing his best to control the panic attack that was trying to break free from inside him.

In the kitchen, Vukasin rushed to the large oven in the corner and pulled open the heavy black door. He reached inside and felt around before ripping out a large blue bag containing several chunky blocks. Opening the bag, he saw the stacks of money inside, and he knew there was more than enough in there to get them set up somewhere new if they were quick enough to make it out of the country. Money can buy you anything you want, except time, and that was the only thing they needed right now.

"LASLO!" he shouted again and turned around to head for the door.

That was when he felt the searing pain in his stomach and saw Laslo was standing directly in front of him, staring right into his eyes.

Vukasin noticed there was no emotion in the younger man's face. He wasn't bearing an expression of fear, or panic, or anything that would have been appropriate for the situation they were in. He wasn't even bearing his usual slightly stupid expression that meant he was daydreaming or deciding what form of abuse to inflict on Jelena today.

He was just cold.

Vukasin looked down to where the pain was coming from and saw the knife embedded in his torso with Laslo's hand wrapped around the handle of the blade. Vukasin was impaled, and the shock of what had happened made him almost as weak as the injury from the knife itself. He tried to speak, but Laslo shook his head, and Vukasin complied, like a beaten dog obeying the order of its cruel master.

Why was this happening? the wounded man thought as the blood started to pool on the part of his shirt that had been penetrated by the weapon. They were a team. They had worked together, and they were supposed to escape together now it was over. *So why was Laslo doing this?*

But Vukasin realised that he already knew the answers to those questions and he cursed himself for not anticipating such a scenario. This was happening because, just like him, Laslo was a cruel, cold-blooded man who was only in it for himself. Just because they worked together, it didn't mean they were friends. Yes, they had been a team, but the second their only source of income had escaped from him at that station, that bond had collapsed. Without Jelena, they were just two greedy, despicable men who would do anything to get ahead. Like murder. Except Laslo had beaten him to it.

The knife was suddenly pulled from his torso and Vukasin felt the air escaping from his lungs. But his next inhalation was met with the second thrust of the knife, then the third.

The bag containing the money fell from Vukasin's hand, and his knees went weak as Laslo continued to drive the knife into his former partner's stomach.

Finally, Vukasin collapsed onto the floor, the sweat on his shirt and jeans from his earlier excursions now replaced by rivers of blood that burst from within him and seeped out across the cold hard tiles of the kitchen.

As he lay dying, Vukasin watched his colleague and murderer pick up the money and store it in his own duffel bag. So that was what it was all about. He just wanted the money for himself. Without Jelena, their income was gone. They could have started again. They could have found another girl. Their contacts in the people-smuggling business would have been able to give them someone else easily enough. There was always another lorry full of illegal immigrants arriving somewhere to be taken advantage of. But Laslo's greed had gotten the better of him, and he was getting out while he could. Vukasin could only wish he had done the same.

He closed his eyes and waited for death to take him. He could feel himself growing weaker by the second, his life draining out of him as quickly as the blood that now surrounded his body. But the sounds of movement around him made him open his eyes for what would probably be the last time. What he saw made him wish that he had kept them closed. It also made him wish for death to come for him sooner.

Laslo was turning on all the gas dials on the cooker.

Not only was he ruthless, but he was also thorough. Burning the place to the ground was certainly one way to get rid of all the fingerprints in the flat, as well as the body that would be left lying amongst them.

Vukasin watched on through blurry, darkening vision as Laslo lit a match and held it up to the grotty curtain that hung down by the side of the kitchen window. The cheap fabric quickly caught light, and the orange flames raced up towards the ceiling. Once the room was filled with gas, the fire would explode and devour every inch of this room and everything inside it. Of course, Laslo would be long gone by that point. He was already carrying the bag containing all their money to the door.

As he opened it, he took one last look at the dying man on the floor of the burning, gaseous room before slamming the door shut behind him and heading for the safety of the street outside.

Left alone to die an inevitable death, all Vukasin could hope for now was that he would succumb to his stab wounds before he succumbed to the explosion that would rip through his body in a couple of moments' time.

Laslo

08:30

Turner Crescent, Brockmore Estate,

North London

Laslo Kovacic closed the front door of the flat he had shared with the man he had just betrayed and pulled a baseball cap down hard over his skull. He turned left, making his way to the nearest tube station, which was a brisk five-minute walk away. From there it was only a short train ride to King's Cross St Pancras Station, where he would purchase a single ticket to Paris before boarding the Eurostar and making the two-hour journey into Europe.

Once in France, he would make contact with the man who had been handling his and Vukasin's operation, explain the situation and discuss how best to proceed from there. Ideally, he would be able to get to Jelena and silence her before she told the police what she knew, but with no idea whereabouts in London, she was that was an impossible task even for him. He had done what he could. Eliminated Vukasin, which was just punishment considering it was he who had lost Jelena. Destroyed the evidence of their stay in the flat, which would happen when the gas was ignited by the flames currently flickering near Vukasin's body. And claimed the most recent proceeds gained from the sex trafficking of Jelena, which would at least go some way to alleviating his employer's concerns. The best and only thing to do now was get out of the country, and there was no time for delay.

"Excuse me."

Laslo heard the woman's voice behind him but decided to keep walking. Whoever it was could mind their own business. The last thing he needed was to show his face to a stranger and end up on an e-fit sketch as the last person seen leaving a burnt-out flat with human remains inside.

"EXCUSE ME!"

The voice was louder now, and just as close. Whoever she was, she was following him.

Laslo's first instinct was to keep his head down and carry on, but it was a tough choice. Such a blatant show of ignoring the stranger's shouting would look suspicious, but turning back would give her a face to describe to the police. He decided to keep walking.

"I LIVE NEXT DOOR TO YOU!"

That was enough to make Laslo stop walking. While he hadn't yet turned around to face the woman behind him, he knew now that he would have to. If she was his neighbour, then she already knew what he looked like, and it was possible that she knew all about his movements and the movements of the other two people who had occupied the flat with him.

He could turn around and politely answer whatever query she had for him. Then he could be on his way again, and there would be no harm done. Well, no harm done, if you excluded the large explosion that was about to rip through this street any moment now.

Laslo turned around and forced a smile onto his pale, sun-deprived face. There might have been a fine start to the summer in London this year, but he had very rarely made the most of it. He tended only to leave the flat at night, either to buy more supplies for him and Vukasin or to visit the casino in Leicester Square where he would gamble away a decent portion of the money he had been earning since he had become a full-time sex trafficker. If he made it to Paris, he would make more of an effort to spend some time outside in the daylight. But he hadn't made it there yet because this stranger was holding him up.

He looked at the woman who had been so desperate to get his attention and was surprised to see that she appeared to be in her seventies or possibly even eighties. Her voice hadn't given away her age, but her grey hair, wrinkled skin and dated fashion sense certainly did. Quite why someone like her was chasing down the street after a 6'5 Serbian man wasn't clear, but if he had to guess then he would assume it was because she had nothing else to do with her time.

A nosy neighbour. A busybody. A retiree sticking her nose into things that didn't concern her. It almost didn't seem worth the delay of waiting to see what it was she wanted, but he had stopped now, and the flat hadn't exploded yet so he could risk a couple of extra seconds to hear what she had to say.

"Was that you making all the noise earlier?" the woman asked him, peering up at the tall man through the thick lenses of her spectacles.

Laslo thought for a moment about what exactly it could be that she was referring to then realised it must be the noise Vukasin had made when he had returned to the flat without Jelena and almost beaten the front door down in his panic.

"Yes. Sorry," Laslo grunted back in his thick Eastern European accent. That was about as chatty as he cared to get with her.

"It was an awful noise. Is everything okay?" she asked again, seemingly believing that whatever had occurred somehow mattered to her and her life today.

Laslo sighed and stared down at the woman. It was no exaggeration to say she was half his size. If he had wanted to, he could probably have picked her up and snapped her in half with his bare hands. Not that he would, although if she held him up any longer, it would become a more appealing possibility.

"Yes," he replied, hoping his short responses would give her a hint that he didn't care to stand here and chat all morning.

"You woke my Albert up," she said, *"He was sleeping by the window, but he jumped awake when you started banging."*

Laslo looked beyond the irritating woman to the flat behind her that was filling with gas. It wouldn't be a tragedy if it exploded now and sent a debris field of bricks towards his neighbour, although it would certainly cause a scene and draw plenty of attention his way. He really needed to be well away from here before it went boom. And he really needed to be on that train to Paris before Jelena told the police where they had kept her.

"Albert's my cat," she went on, somehow thinking that the man she was talking to cared about such trivial things.

"Sorry," Laslo said and turned away to continue walking. Surely the old woman would get the message now that he didn't want to talk.

"How is your friend?" she called after him, and despite every part of his body wanting to keep moving in the opposite direction to her, he had to know what she meant by that.

Had she heard something? Did she know what he had done? Or worse, was she stalling him because she had already called the police and they were on their way over here right now to arrest him and break into the flat that contained evidence of all his crimes?

Laslo took a deep breath and turned around again. He knew he was unlikely to make it to the underground station before the flat exploded now. He probably wouldn't even make it off the same street in time. Eyewitnesses would describe a large bang and seeing a tall, white man in a blue baseball cap fleeing the scene of the fire. Just what he needed. But that was a problem for the next moment. He had one to deal with right now in the shape of the irritating woman standing in front of him on the street.

"My friend?" he asked.

"The young girl I see leaving your flat every morning. Dark hair. Dreadfully skinny. Is everything alright with her?"

Laslo knew, of course, that she was referring to Jelena and was somewhat alarmed by the fact that she knew the time of day they tended to move her. She had probably been keeping an eye on them for a while.

Why couldn't people mind their own business?

He and Vukasin had certainly kept themselves to themselves since they had begun renting the flat five months earlier. They had made sure not to speak with any of their neighbours, not to make any loud noises that might arouse suspicion or complaints, and certainly not to make a big show of the kidnapped woman they had forced into prostitution almost every day since they had pulled her from that lorry from Belgrade. But this woman had obviously been keeping an eye on them, most likely from the window of the flat she shared with her stupid cat. She knew all their faces, and she had even noticed that Jelena looked frail.

What else did she know and, more importantly, what else was she going to tell the police when they arrived and put the flames out on Vukasin's burning body?

"She is sick," Laslo said, a plan quickly forming in his mind. *"Do you have medicine? She has bad headache, and fever."*

The old woman thought about this for a second.

"Can you not take her to a doctor?" she asked, her face now a wrinkled expression of concern about the poor girl she had been spying on all this time.

"We try to get from doctor but they say we need to do paperwork," Laslo explained, *"We're on visas. They won't give us medicine."*

"That's terrible. They'd rather let a poor girl go sick then help you," she said, shaking her head. *"That's Brexit, I guess. Everyone for themselves. Terrible if you*

ask me. My husband Charles, god rest his soul. He fought in the war, and if he was here now, it would make him sick to see the world the way it is today."

Laslo nodded. The street hadn't turned into a blazing pile of bricks yet, and he began to wonder if something had gone wrong with his plan. But the fire had definitely taken hold when he had left, and the gas was turned on. Nothing could stop that place going up. *So why hadn't it exploded yet?*

"Do you have medicine we could use?" he asked her, *"It would really help."*

"Of course. I have a cupboard full of pills. What does she have? Is it sickness or flu?"

"Flu, I think," he said and started to lead the woman subconsciously back towards her flat - the same flat that was beside the imminent pile of rubble.

"I can help you. But you do know you can buy these things from the supermarket."

"I didn't know."

"That's okay, you know for next time."

Now it was she who was leading him towards her flat, and Laslo knew then that if the next thirty seconds went to plan, he would have taken care of his second witness of the day.

They reached her front door, and she took the key from her cardigan pocket. Her hand was shaking, but she eventually slid the key into the lock and opened up.

"Do you want me to wait here?" Laslo said to her as she stepped inside.

"Yes, that's fine, I'll be one minute," she said and walked away into her home, leaving her door

slightly ajar behind her and unwittingly facilitating the next step of Laslo's plan.

He stepped inside and closed the door.

He took note of his surroundings. The antiquated furniture. The mantelpiece that was full of black and white photos of the old lady and her late husband. And the black cat sitting on the windowsill basking in the beam of sunlight that had found its way through the tall block of flats that littered this estate and made it into her home.

It was small but pleasant and certainly more homely than the flat he and Vukasin had kept Jelena in next door. But there wasn't time for note-taking. He was aware of the impending carnage that was about to unfold on the other side of the wall he was standing next to, so he went quickly about the next part of his plan.

Moments later, Laslo Kovacic closed the front door of the flat belonging to the elderly lady he had just strangled and crossed the street, putting distance between himself and the flat that would erupt any second now. He had made sure to position her dead body against the wall closest to where the fire was burning, so it would bear the full brunt of the explosion when it came. He had smelt the gas and could even see deep black patches forming on the floral wallpaper of the old woman's home, a sure sign of the inferno that had taken hold only metres away.

He neared the end of the street and thought about pausing to watch the explosion from a safe distance, but he kept going, aware that time was against him. He didn't know the timetable for the trains to Paris and worried there might be a long wait at St Pancras Station if he were to arrive in between services. If necessary, then he would call his handler while he waited and explain the situation. But ideally, he wouldn't have to wait long for the train and could make the call while he was in motion, just before he lost signal as the train entered the Channel Tunnel.

Suddenly the explosion came, and it was just as loud as Laslo had imagined it would be. But he didn't turn back to see the large dark plumes of smoke filtering up into the clear blue sky. He just carried on walking whilst listening to the sound of numerous car alarms blaring, no doubt triggered by the shockwaves from the blast that had ravaged the street.

Soon this area would be filled with the sounds of sirens from the emergency service vehicles that would be deployed after several frantic 999 calls from terrified members of the public, who were looking at the pile of rubble where a row of flats had once stood.

The fire crews would work hard to put the flames out. The paramedics would offer their assistance, although there would be nothing they could do for the charred and barely identifiable bodies retrieved from the scene. And lastly, the police officers would begin their investigations into what had caused a quiet street on a council estate in North London to suddenly resemble a war zone and why at least two people had lost their lives on this warm summer's morning.

All signs would point to a gas leak and the victims being two unlucky souls who were just in the wrong place at the wrong time. That would be until

Jelena returned to show the police officers the place where she had been kept for four months, and they would then begin to suspect that the explosion was not caused by bad luck at all.

But by then, Laslo would be in a different part of Europe and with nothing tying him to the scene he had made sure was destroyed, he would be free to carry on his life of crime. But as he arrived at the tube station and left behind the bright sunshine for the dark shadows of the Underground, he knew one thing for sure. Jelena was the only one that could tie him to the kidnapping, and the abuse, and the explosion, and the two dead bodies in the burnt-out flats. So just like he had eliminated those witnesses, one day he would make sure to come back and eliminate her too.

Alicia

08:31

Camden Police Station, North London

Alicia Shaw was only ten minutes away from finishing her shift, but ten minutes was a long time in the life of a 999 emergency call handler.

It had been a long night, consisting of a lot of hard work, some stressful moments and a few laughs with her colleagues, but now she was thoroughly ready to call it a day and go home to bed. There would be only a few more calls to deal with, but in this line of work, it was impossible to predict the nature of them.

"Police emergency. Go ahead operator" she said into her headset, as the next call was put through to her.

"Connecting mobile 07882 939211" came the voice of the operator, who had already ascertained that this call was to be directed to the police, rather than to the fire or ambulance services.

"Thank you, go ahead caller you are through to the police," Alicia said, her fingers poised over her keyboard to record every detail that she was about to hear.

"Err, yes, I'm waiting for the number 57 bus, but it hasn't turned up yet, and I'm going to be late for work," said the male voice on the other end of the line.

Alicia paused to make sure she had heard the man correctly.

"You've called the police to report that your bus hasn't turned up?" Alicia said, shaking her head so much her headset wobbled. She saw her colleague Ruth put her palm to her face opposite her.

"Yeah it was due half an hour ago, but there's no sign of it and I don't know what to do," the man said, sounding stressed and somehow oblivious to his stupidity.

"Sir, you do not call this number to report your bus being late. We do not deal with things like this" Alicia said in her most calm, professional manner.

"But what do I do?" he asked her again, not taking on board anything he had just been told.

"You are aware you have called the emergency services?" Alicia replied, her finger poised over the key that would end the call instantly should she push it.

"Well yes but..."

"This is not an emergency, is it, sir?"

There was a stony silence on the other end of the phone.

"This is not an emergency, is it, sir?" she repeated.

"Well no, I guess not but-"

"I'm going to clear the line now, so it's free for emergency calls."

Alicia ended the call and raised her eyebrows at her friend across the desk.

"Can you believe that?" Alicia said, taking a swig from her water bottle and glancing at the clock.

Ruth shrugged and began a new call of her own, one which was hopefully more relevant to their line of work.

The crazy thing was that that wasn't even the most ridiculous call Alicia had taken during her shift. A woman had called her just after 6 am, almost hysterical because she had forgotten the password for her laptop. Alicia had been forced to explain that the police don't deal with I.T. issues and that calling the emergency response line to report such problems was a complete waste of their time. Astonishingly, despite this explanation, the caller had still failed to see the error of her ways and had insisted that she needed to be put through to somebody urgently. Maybe, heaven forbid, she had entered the wrong password so many times that she had been locked out for half an hour. Alicia wondered what would happen if this lady's computer lost power? Then it really would be an emergency. Both the police and the ambulance services would have to be summoned.

Or not.

Alicia raised her hands above her head and stretched the muscles in her upper body. When she was done here, it would be home to bed, followed by an hour at the gym, a healthy meal and a quick catch up with her partner Jeff, before she returned for her fourth and final night shift of this week's rota. After some time off, she would be back to day shifts, giving her the opportunity to catch up on her social life, which always suffered when she spent her weekend evenings manning the phones. But that was the job she had signed up for.

She was just about to reach for her water again when the next call came.

"Police emergency. Go ahead, operator."

"Connecting landline 020 7572 6299."

"Thank you, go ahead caller you are through to the police."

"Err, yes, hello" spoke the woman on the other end of the line.

"What's your emergency?" Alicia asked calmly.

"There was a man outside my house threatening me and trying to get in."

"Okay, is the man still there now?"

"Yes, I think he's gone around the back."

"Okay, can I have your postcode please?"

"Yes, it's N1 0PA."

Alicia's fingers moved quickly across the keyboard.

"Okay, is that number 35 Churchill Way?"

"That's right."

"Okay, and what's your name?"

"Michelle."

"Okay Michelle, and you say you can't see the man at the moment."

"No."

"Do you know the man?"

"Yes, he's my ex-boyfriend."

Alicia entered the information into the system as quickly as she received it.

"Okay I can see we have another unit in the area for a call out to a disturbance, I believe this is referring to the same person;"

"Yes, I think he's been round to the neighbour's house too."

"That's right. The officers should be there on your street any minute now."

"Okay."

"Michelle, can you stay in your house until the officers have checked the area and confirmed it is safe for you to leave?"

"Yes, that's fine."

"Thank you."

Alicia looked across to her colleague Matt who she could see had handled the call from the neighbour moments before hers had come in. He gave her the thumbs up.

"Okay, Michelle, the officers should be arriving now."

"I can see them outside."

"That's great."

"He's talking to them."

"Who's talking to them?"

"My ex. He's back outside the house."

"Okay, just stay where you are for the moment."

"I will."

Alicia paused for a moment, allowing time for the events outside the house to play out before checking back in again with the caller.

"The officers will come and speak to you shortly but for now is there anything else you need to tell me?"

"No, that's it. Thank you."

"Thank you."

Alicia ended the call and completed her records in the log. Routine calls such as that were common during her shifts. Ex-partners trying to get back into their home after being thrown out for something they may or may not have done. Of course, there was the potential for violence but more often than not the person attempting to gain entry backed down the second the police arrived. It was all routine, and Alicia saw she only had a few more minutes left of her shift.

She looked across at Ruth who was in the middle of a call of her own, as were most of her colleagues. It was a typically busy time. Weekends were always the worst, but there was never what one would call a quiet period in this job. Situations were fluid, ever-changing, constantly springing up, so whatever time of day it was, all emergency responders had to be ready for action at any second.

There was a saying in this job:

When the shit hits the fan, make sure you're not downwind.

It may have been a crude phrase, but it was true that when the inevitable nightmarish calls came into the call centre, most handlers would prefer not to be one of the ones to answer them. But Alicia tried not to see it like that.

She had been employed as a call handler for the police for almost three years now, and she enjoyed her work. Even the night shifts could be tolerated, and they at least gave her weeks a little more variety than she had experienced before in the classic nine-to-five routine. The jobs she had held in retail and administration during her early twenties had left her unfulfilled, and she had been on the lookout for something a little more challenging when she had seen a television advertisement calling for emergency call handlers.

The advert itself was cleverly constructed, drawing the viewer in immediately with the sound of a child's voice over a black screen asking for help after his mummy had fallen down the stairs at home. The call handler then asked the child if their parent was conscious, only to get the cute but worrying response that their mummy was asleep. The situation seemed tense, but through the calm and clever prompts from the operator, the child was able to provide all the information necessary to get the emergency services to the address in time. The first time she had seen the advert, Alicia had initially assumed it was going to conclude with a message about the importance of teaching your children to call 999 in emergencies, but that wasn't the case. The caption on screen after the call had simply said "Could you have taken this call?" before a final shot showed the Metropolitan Police logo and the website to visit for anyone interested in becoming a call handler for the emergency services.

For some reason, the advert had stuck with Alicia and when she saw the second one, which featured a call from a terrified woman who had locked herself in her bathroom while her abusive partner tried to get to her, she felt compelled to seek further information. After visiting the website and learning more about the role of an emergency call handler, she had decided to take a chance and apply.

There were a few pre-requisites for the job, like good typing skills and the ability to remain calm, but nothing too unobtainable and overall, it seemed like the ability to work in a fast-paced team environment was the main skill required.

After passing the necessary security checks and undergoing numerous scenario-based training exercises, Alicia had eventually gained full-time employment as a Communications Officer with the Metropolitan Police. The job was based in the North London Borough of Camden, but the organisation ran the policing operations for Greater London and handled an estimated 13,000 calls a day. It was safe to say that Alicia was yet to experience a dull shift.

On only her second day in the job, she had taken a call from a woman who had very calmly explained to her that she had killed her husband and wanted to know if she could put the kettle on for the officers that were soon going to be on the way to her address. But if she thought that was strange, the time that had passed since had taught her one thing:

Expect the unexpected.

She had no way of knowing exactly how many calls she had handled in the time she had been working for the police, but the thing that always amazed her was that not a week went by when she wasn't faced with something she hadn't encountered before. There had been violent incidents ranging from murder to sexual abuse and assault. There had been crimes underway at the time, like robberies, public disturbances and threats to life. And, of course, the bizarre incidents, such as the time when someone called to report that McDonald's had run out of ketchup, or when the caller had demanded a police escort to the airport so they wouldn't miss their flight. A man had even called on the 1st of January just to wish her a Happy New Year.

It was a crazy job, and Alicia often thought you had to be slightly crazy yourself to do it every day, but there was no doubting its importance and value to society. The older she got, the more she realised job satisfaction was important and despite having some truly bad days and being witness to some horrific crimes, she knew that what she was doing was having a direct impact in her community and not many people could say that about their line of work.

Another call came in, and Alicia prepared herself for what would be the last one of her shift.

"Police emergency. Go ahead operator" she said, ensuring she was as alert and ready as she had been for the first call that she had taken almost twelve hours earlier.

"Connecting landline 020 7429 3182."

"Thank you. Go ahead caller. You are through to the police."

"There's been an explosion on my street," said the shaky voice of the elderly gentlemen at the other end of the line.

"Did you say an explosion?" Alicia asked, aware of how important it was to clarify key details as early as possible to avoid any confusion further down the line.

"Yes, the flat opposite me has exploded," the man said, sounding a little out of breath.

"Are you okay, sir?" Alicia asked.

"Well my downstairs window smashed, and I almost had a bloody heart attack but apart from that I'm fine," came the curt response down the phone,

drawing a small smile from Alicia despite the apparent seriousness of the call.

"Can I take your postcode, please?"

"N1 2DQ."

"Okay, is that number 73 Turner Crescent?"

"That's right."

"Okay, and what is your name, sir?"

"George."

"Okay George, I can see that there are a large number of emergency response units already on their way to that area now."

"Well that doesn't surprise me, you could have heard the bang in South London."

"Can you tell me what happened, George?"

"Yes, of course. I was upstairs in my bedroom trying to find my cufflinks. I have a dinner to attend this evening you see, and I need my cufflinks for my suit. It's for my bowls club. I'm on the committee."

Alicia couldn't help but smile again but maintained her concentration at the same time.

"You said the flat across the street exploded?"

"Yes, I was looking out on my street when it went up. Terrifying it was. Flames as red as hell. The building is almost levelled. I hope nobody was inside."

"The fire and ambulance crews will be there any second now. This is the line for the police," Alicia said, having yet to ascertain his reason for requesting the police over the fire service. But it wasn't uncommon in events like this for a member of the public to ask for the wrong service during times of distress or shock.

"Yes, I know that," George snapped back, *"It's about my neighbour."*

"Your neighbour?"

"Yes, the man who lived in the flat that just blew up."

"Okay, what's his name?"

"I don't know. I never spoke to him. He kept to himself. They all did actually. There were three of them living there."

"Do you know if they were inside when the explosion occurred?" Alicia asked, hoping to glean some vitally important information that she could pass on to the fire services as they sped towards the site of the explosion.

"I know one of them wasn't because I saw him walking away just before it exploded," George said, his breathing now a little more controlled than it had been at the start of the conversation.

"Okay, so he isn't hurt?" Alicia attempted to confirm.

"No he's fine," George answered. *"But it's very odd."*

"What's odd?"

"Well if you were walking down a street and a flat exploded behind you, what would you do?" he asked her, momentarily turning the tables on her.

"I suppose I would run away from it," Alicia replied.

"Yes, of course. But before that, when you first heard it, what would you do?"

Alicia wasn't sure where he was going with this, and she was just about to remind him that unless he had information about an emergency situation, then she needed to keep this line clear, when he answered his question for her.

"You would turn around and look, wouldn't you?" he said to her.

"Yes, I suppose I would," Alicia replied.

"Well that's the thing," George said, wheezing slightly down the phone. *"This man didn't turn around at all. He just kept on walking away. He didn't even flinch. Does that not seem odd to you?"*

Alicia thought about it for a second and tried to come up with a rational explanation as to why someone wouldn't react to an explosion in their vicinity. Perhaps the man was deaf. But by the sounds of it, this explosion would have shaken the whole street. Deaf or not, he would have at least felt it. So what other reason could there be for him not turning around and looking?

"You say this man lived at the address?"

"That's right."

"Could you describe him?"

"Yes. Late twenties. Tall. Thin. He was wearing a blue baseball cap."

"And what direction was he going in?" Alicia asked as her fingers danced across the keyboard in front of her.

"East. Towards Euston."

"Okay, thank you," Alicia said, entering the information into the system.

"Do you think it's unusual?" George asked her.

"Unusual?" Alicia responded, glancing at the flurry of activity on her monitor screen that showed the radar for the area where the explosion had occurred.

The more she thought about it, the more she did think it was unusual. And this just summed up her job perfectly. There she was, only moments from finishing her night shift and now she was processing information for what was seemingly a massive incident at a flat in North London, involving all three emergency services, with potential casualties and structural damage. To top it off, a resident of the affected flat was seen leaving the scene just before the event and had not exhibited the kind of reaction that one would expect from someone who had just heard his home exploding.

It was going to be a busy morning for the fire crews, the ambulance services and definitely for the police.

When the shit hits the fan, make sure you're not downwind.

Louise

08:32

Waterloo, Central London

Louise Robertson stared at the police station across the street and promised herself she would go back over there in one minute's time. She knew that if she didn't, then she would regret it. But she couldn't help wondering whether she might regret it if she did go.

Basically, she had no idea what to do.

The day had started as normal. She had boarded her tube train in Kilburn Park and travelled down the Bakerloo line to Waterloo. As had become her habit, she had stolen from one of her fellow passengers on the way, this time taking a purse from a woman's handbag as she stood directly behind her. From Waterloo, she would eventually go to her workplace, the offices of Z3 Group, a digital design company where she worked as a receptionist. But first, she planned to visit Waterloo Police Station.

Instead of turning left out of the train station, she had turned right and, following the directions on her mobile phone, she had made her way through the busy streets to the building bearing the Metropolitan Police sign. It had taken her another five minutes of procrastinating before she had walked up the steps to the entrance and a further two minutes at the top before she had pushed open the heavy glass doors and gone inside.

It had been her first time in a police station, and she hadn't been sure what to expect. Her only knowledge of places like that came from films and television shows. She expected there to be a crowded waiting room full of victims of crime, all looking afraid and broken as they waited to be called to a witness room by an officer wearing a black and white uniform and a stern expression. She had expected there to be several officers manning a front desk, drowning in a sea of paperwork and struggling to handle the constant stream of criminals, witnesses and colleagues approaching their station. She might even have expected to see a hardened criminal being led past her in handcuffs, flanked on either side by two burly officers, while a weary detective in a long coat followed them to an interrogation room, carrying a folder full of evidence.

But there hadn't been any of that when she had stepped inside Waterloo Police Station. Instead of a crowded waiting room, there were just a couple of unoccupied chairs. Instead of an overwhelmed front desk, there had been just one elderly lady sitting behind a screen. And there definitely hadn't been any criminals being marched past her in handcuffs or any sign of the type of detectives she was used to seeing in Netflix documentaries. In fact, if it hadn't been for the woman behind the glass screen wearing a police uniform, she would have assumed she was in the wrong place entirely.

Louise turned her head away from the window that overlooked the police station and gazed down at the steaming cup of coffee sitting on the table in front of her. She raised the cup to her mouth, took a sip and felt the warm liquid move soothingly down her throat. Cappuccinos were her go-to drink when she felt stressed. She used vodka in the same way, but it was a little early for that, and none of the pubs and bars around here were open yet. Maybe she would get something stronger at lunchtime, but for now, coffee would have to do.

The coffee shop was typically crowded for this time of day, as dozens of commuters filtered in and out to get their fix of caffeine before heading to the office. She had done well to secure herself a seat, such was the volume of people in here, and she had been particularly pleased to get one by the window. Sitting here, with the early morning sunshine filtering through the glass and warming her skin, it would be tempting to think that all was right with her world. But all it took was another glance at the ominous brick building across the street, and the coat of arms of the London police constabulary displayed proudly beside it to remind her that she had troubling reasons for being here.

When she had stepped into the station and realised it was nothing like she had expected it to be, she hadn't been entirely sure what to do and had simply stood awkwardly by the front door looking around and doubting her decision. That was until the woman behind the front desk had looked up from her computer screen and addressed her.

"Can I help you?" she had asked, seeming surprisingly chirpy for the time of day. Either she had just started her shift and was full of energy from her breakfast, or she was just about to finish and was full of the excitement at the prospect of home.

Louise had forced her reluctant body closer to the desk until she stood in front of the Perspex window, looking down at the seated police officer on the other side.

"Hi, erm...my name's Louise," she had said, unsure how to introduce what she wanted to say.

"Hi Louise," the officer had replied, smiling, yet somehow maintaining an air of defensiveness as she waited to hear what the young woman in front of her was about to tell her.

That defensiveness probably made sense, Louise had thought at the time. All sorts of people must walk into police stations with something to report. Sometimes they were the victims, but sometimes they were the perpetrators. They could be there in the role of a good citizen, trying to pass on a piece of information that may or may not be useful to an investigation. Or they could be a lunatic, owning up to a truly horrific crime or even intent on committing more. The Perspex barrier was definitely a good idea, as was the police officer's guarded demeanour as she waited to find out what this next part of her job was going to involve.

"Erm..." Louise had stalled at that point and looked behind the officer at the room she was sitting in. Barring some files on a trolley, a computer monitor on a

desk and a slow clock on the wall there didn't seem to be much back there.

"I'm here to report a crime," she had eventually managed to say.

"Okay," the officer had said calmly while reaching for a piece of paper attached to a clipboard. *"And what is the nature of the crime?"*

It was said in such a relaxed manner, but inside Louise had felt anything but relaxed.

"Erm..."

She had known it would be tough to say the words. Hell, it was tough just saying them to herself in her head never mind to somebody else, especially somebody in a police uniform. She knew she would have to say them eventually, but whether it was her hesitation or her general demeanour, the female officer had just smiled and slid the clipboard through the gap in the window.

"Don't worry, just fill out your details on this form, and I will get an officer to come and speak to you as soon as possible," she said.

Louise had felt immediate relief at being granted a few more minutes' reprieve before having to talk about why she was there. She had smiled at the officer, who must have picked up on her gratitude at not being pressured to talk because she smiled back and said *"Just take a seat, and someone will be with you shortly."*

Louise had made her way to one of the plastic chairs, thinking about how it felt almost like she was in a doctor's surgery or waiting for a job interview. But she knew her reasons for being here, and there was no forgetting them, no matter how hard the woman on the front desk was trying to put her at ease.

When she had taken her seat, she had looked at the information on the paper attached to the clipboard and seen that it was just a standard form, asking for basic details like name, date of birth and address. It would all have looked pretty banal if it hadn't been for the logo of the Met Police printed at the top of the page reminding her how serious what she was about to do really was.

She had used the pen she had been given to fill in her details.

Name: **Louise Robertson**

Age: **27**

Address...

Louise had worked her way through the form easily enough until she had reached the part where it asked for information about her reason for being there today. There was a box to tick to indicate if you were the victim of a crime and her pen had hovered over it, inches from the paper, unable to complete its task.

She had looked below the box and seen that there was a much larger one to be completed, this one asking for details of the crime. That had been as far as she had got. Because she had known then that if she couldn't even fill in the box to say what had happened to her, then there was no way she would be able to say the words to somebody and definitely no way she would be able to testify about it in a court of law.

After that realisation, she had stood up quickly, removed the paper from the clipboard and rushed out of the door before the officer on the front desk had even had the chance to call after her.

That had been almost fifteen minutes ago, and now here she was, sitting in the coffee shop across the road from the station, still deliberating whether to go back over there or to just take her coffee and go to work. If she hurried, she could still make it in time for her 9 am start. But that would mean that her ex-boyfriend would go another day without facing the consequences of his actions and that thought was just as unbearable as the prospect of sitting in a room with a concerned officer, recounting her version of events of that fateful night four months earlier.

She was a rape victim. She had at least admitted it to herself, if not to anybody else quite yet. And she knew that not only did she owe it to herself to report the crime and seek justice, but that she owed it to the other women with whom her ex-boyfriend might come into contact.

So why was it so hard to speak to the police about it? Why was it so hard to speak to anybody about it?

Realising she wasn't making it any easier for herself to go back to the station by thinking like this, she suddenly remembered about the purse she had stolen on her tube journey earlier that morning. Pulling it out of her summer coat pocket, she laid it on the table and studied it for a moment. It was a dark red Mulberry purse and would have cost its owner around £150. Louise knew that because she had spent plenty of time online with various Mulberry purses in her shopping basket and her finger hovering over the buy button. But she had never actually bought one, the fear of not having enough money left over at the end of the month for more important things like rent and food being the main reason for her reluctance.

But now that she had one in her possession, it was nice to spend a couple of moments experiencing it. The smooth leather surface. The gold-coloured zip that ran across the top. The imprinted lettering of the purse's brand across the front. It was beautiful. Much nicer than her own purse, which was currently sitting somewhere at the bottom of her overcrowded, disorganised handbag on the table beside her coffee.

But unlike most thieves, she hadn't taken it because she wanted something she couldn't afford. She had taken it because stealing had become her way of distracting herself from the trauma of what she had experienced at the hands of a man she had once trusted. So, before the memories of what he had done to her could infiltrate her mind again, she quickly unzipped the purse and fingered through the contents.

There was a purple and blue Visa debit card, with the name Manuela Hughes printed across the bottom. There was an orange and red Monzo card bearing the same name, as well as a white and black access card for CityLife Gym. The driver's licence bore a photo of the woman from whom Louise had stolen on the front, although she looked a lot younger in the image than she had done on the train today. Finally, in another compartment of the purse, there was a bundle of receipts, a ten-pound note and lastly, in a small zip, some pieces of small change.

The contents were standard, but it was what she could do with them later that excited Louise the most. With a name and image, she could learn everything about the woman through social media. Her profession. Her relationship status. Her last holiday location. What she did at weekends. Who she did it with. That was the best thing about stealing for Louise. Because as long as she was engrossed in the life of a stranger, she could avoid thinking about her ex-boyfriend and the assault he had inflicted on her.

She felt the warmth of the sunlight momentarily disappear and, looking out of the window, noticed that a large cloud had obscured the sun in what was an otherwise clear, blue sky. Her eyes then lowered to the large building across the street, and she knew that today would not be the day that she reported Joe Swan for being a rapist.

She felt sick because she knew he was probably out there now, chatting up a pretty girl on his way into work or perhaps looking forward to a date with someone he had met online. But she also felt a strong sense of relief that she wouldn't have to recount her experience to anybody today. She would go to work, regroup and regather, and make another attempt to report it tomorrow. Or the next day. If she couldn't do it in person, she could always do it on the police website. Or through a friend or family member. She had options.

She just didn't want to think about any of them right now.

Louise took the ten-pound note out of the stolen purse and held it in her palm as she gathered her possessions and stood up from her table by the window. She squeezed past some of the other people in the shop, manoeuvred herself around the long queue that snaked back from the front counter, then broke out onto the warm, busy street.

From there, she headed in the direction of her office, and away from the police station, only stopping for a moment to hand the ten-pound note to the homeless man she had seen sitting in the doorway of a disused retail store on her way past earlier that morning.

She gave the money to him because he seemed like a good man. But she was well aware that appearances could be deceptive.

After all, Joe had seemed like a good man and look how wrong she had been there.

Joe

08:33

Borough High Street, Central London

Joe Swan knew his date with April was going well. A number of things had given him this positive impression, such as the fact that she kept touching her hair while they spoke. Every self-respecting lothario knew that subconscious grooming was a sure-fire sign of physical attraction. The fact that she had laughed at his many attempts at humour was another good indicator that she was enjoying getting to know him. But most convincing of all, they had been in discussion for half an hour now, and the conversation had never once threatened to run dry. The time had passed in the blink of an eye, and you know what they say about that.

Time flies when you're having fun.

So far, they had discussed many of the usual topics that tend to come up on a first date. Like what they did for work:

"I'm a Sales Advisor at Barringdon Insurers," he had told her, flashing the expensive watch on his wrist as he had picked up his coffee cup and taken a long sip. *"I was one of the lucky ones who made it through the trainee scheme. The plan is to get into selling life insurance. That's where the real money is."*

"I'm a project coordinator at Five Star Interiors," she had said, fiddling with her own coffee cup and

checking on her hair again. *"You probably haven't heard of it. It's quite a small company. It's boring, but it's okay, I guess."*

They had discussed where and with whom they lived in London:

"I rent with a mate from work and a guy from my 5-a-side footy team," he had said, brushing his hands across his neatly trimmed stubble and making sure she got a good glimpse of his watch again. *"It's a typical lad's pad, but I'll probably try and get my own place soon. I'll be earning enough once I get my promotion."*

She had smiled. *"I live in Angel with my best friend Katie,"* she told him, whilst fidgeting with one of her rings and doing her best to go five seconds without touching her hair. *"I love it there, there are so many cool pubs. It's great in the summer."*

And of course, they had discussed a few of their hobbies and interests:

"Football, rugby, golf, drinking with the boys," he had confessed to her, before realising that he probably wasn't selling himself too well and so threw in the more general *"and going to the cinema, watching Netflix, just chilling out, you know?"*

"I love the gym," she had said. He suspected that this was a lie but couldn't be sure as she looked in decent enough shape. *"And just the usual things, you know, like drinks with friends and chilling out."*

He had made her laugh with tales of his previous dating disasters, like the time he had got himself locked in the toilet of the pub they were in with no phone signal and by the time he had got out, the girl had gone, convinced he had stood her up. She had some pretty funny stories herself, like going on a date with a guy who turned out to be a massive Star Wars nerd and got the barista to write something weird and geeky on her coffee cup in Starbucks. And they'd even each had time to mention where they originally came from.

"Orpington," he had said, referring to the leafy town in Kent where he had been born. *"My parents and most of my mates are still there, but I don't think I could ever move back. I love the city too much."*

"Chelmsford," she had told him. Essex was not a part of the country that he knew, so his perception of Chelmsford was based purely on what he had gleaned from the reality television show *The Only Way Is Essex*.

"It's nothing like the television show," she had quickly clarified, clearly used to people forming inaccurate opinions as a result of the popular programme.

All in all, it had been a fun meeting between two strangers with plenty of laughter and zero awkward moments. That was all he could have asked for considering it was a first date in a coffee shop early on a Monday morning.

He found April extremely attractive, though he had already known that because he had seen her photo on Tinder a couple of days earlier. He was partial to blondes, though he didn't care if they were blonde, brunette, red-headed or even shaven-headed as long as they looked good. But when he had first arrived at the coffee shop and seen her sitting at the table by the window, with the early morning sunlight dancing across her face, he had realised she looked even better in person than in her profile photo. As he had made his way to the table to meet her, he knew before a word had been spoken that he would consider himself very lucky if their interactions were to result in them being in the bedroom together.

But once they had got past the initial greeting, Joe had been happy to discover that April was just as exciting in the personality department as she was in the looks department. She had told him how this early morning dating thing was new for her and was a sort of trial run. When she had confessed that she usually preferred her dates to involve multiple bottles of prosecco in a bar with a good atmosphere, he could tell she was up for fun and that if he did well enough to get a second date with her, it would likely be a lot boozier and raunchier than this one.

He had done well to highlight what he considered to be his assets during the date. Like his rugged handsomeness, defined by the perfect amount of facial hair that he had grown for today, which made him look more masculine than scruffy. Like the fact that he was gainfully employed and had turned up in his best dark blue shirt and tie, a look that had so far proved most successful with the ladies. And like the fact that he was making good money for someone his age, which he had strategically displayed by flashing his watch, his new mobile phone and his wallet, all at discreet but purposeful times during their chat. He'd even managed to avoid being caught taking glances at her chest when she spoke, instead taking the opportunities when she had looked out of the window or down at her coffee cup. He really had been a proper gentleman for the last half an hour. But now the date was almost over, and all he had to do was make sure he secured the next one.

"I'm sorry, I need to get going for work," April said, glancing at her phone screen. *"Another boring day in the office awaits."*

"Phone in sick and let's go get a proper drink," he cheekily replied, only half-joking.

She laughed and rolled her eyes, and he was struck again by how attracted he was to her.

"I wish. I've got so many deadlines this week. But we should go for that drink soon," she said, which was music to Joe's ears.

"Okay, but on one condition," he said, deliberately holding back on the next part to draw out the suspense and build the sexual tension that was already forming between them.

"Oh yeah, what's that?" she asked, smiling curiously.

"I pick the place next time. And the start time. No offence, but I reckon I can come up with somewhere a bit wilder than Caffe Nero on a Monday morning."

April laughed again, her long hair flowing backwards as she tilted her head.

"I'm sure you can. It would be a massive fail if you couldn't."

They shared a flirtatious glance then he reluctantly stood up, followed closely by April. They walked through the busy coffee shop to the door, passing the queue of bleary-eyed commuters who were waiting for their caffeine and sugar fix from the harassed girl behind the counter.

Joe held open the door for April, and they stepped outside onto the sun-kissed pavement of one of the busiest streets in Central London.

"So you'd better get to work, and I'd better get working on where I'm taking you next time then," he said to her as they stood beside each other in a sea of swirling pedestrians and car horns.

"Sounds like a plan," she replied, turning away and slowly increasing the distance between them. *"Text me when you think of a good idea. And when your head has stopped hurting."*

She gave him a cheeky wink, and he laughed as he watched her walk away, her blonde head bobbing beside all the other people that were competing for space in this frenetic part of London.

When she was out of sight, he allowed himself a small fist pump at the successful outcome of the date before turning and walking in the opposite direction towards London Bridge. He didn't have to be in the office until 09:30, so decided to make the half-hour walk to his office in Tower Bridge instead of jumping on the tube and missing out on the sunshine.

He smiled to himself as he joined the flow of commuters streaming in the same direction as him, and thought through a couple of options for where he could take April for their second date. A few places came to mind straight away.

Itzy's was a trendy wine bar near his office where he had spent many a fun night, and he was sure she would be impressed with the atmosphere in there. But then he remembered he had had a thing with one of the barmaids there and quickly decided that it was a no-go area for a little while longer.

Passion Bar was an option. It was a new bar that had recently opened near Liverpool Street, and he had heard good things. Plus, he was sure she wouldn't have been there yet, and it would be better if he showed her somewhere new. It would make the date more exciting for them both if they were on unfamiliar territory.

Then again it might be better to play it safe and just do a little bar crawl, starting somewhere simple like All Bar One, where he would be more relaxed as it was somewhere he had drunk in hundreds of times over the last couple of years. But that was the plain, average choice and if he had picked up on one thing from April during their date, it was that she had wasn't the type of girl that did plain or average.

Passion Bar it was.

Joe caught sight of the water cutting through the city and left the craziness of Borough behind for the equal craziness of the large bridge that stretched over the River Thames. On a sunny day, there weren't many prettier views of London than this one. Today the deep-blue sky helped brighten the murky waters of the river and made it look more appealing than it usually did. The modern architecture on either side of the water glistened in response to the brilliant sunshine, appearing even more majestic than usual. But the best thing about days like this was the mindset they put Londoners in. People who were used to rushing over this bridge in a foul mood while often being battered by high winds and torrential rain were instead able to slow down a little and appreciate their walk into work when the weather was being kinder to them. Things seemed to be more peaceful here when the sun was out, and Joe could sense the optimism in the air as he made his way over the bridge.

It was views like this that had helped him decide that he could never go back to small-town suburban living. He wanted to be here, with the skyscrapers, and the crowds, and the numerous bars, restaurants, clubs and clubbers. London was where the action was, and the money. Sure, it had its downsides. The tube sucked. Prices were high. And the threat of terrorism lurked at the back of the minds of everyone who spent time here, himself included. The sight of the barriers at both ends of the bridge were evidence of that, installed after a vehicle attack on pedestrians only a few years earlier. But it was days like today when London felt more powerful than any of that. It was his new home, and he felt extremely lucky to be able to say that.

He paused for a moment and took out his phone, suddenly feeling the need to capture a record of his walk into the office on this beautiful June morning. He took a great photo, the Thames in the foreground stretching all the way back to Tower Bridge in the background, and he was just about to upload it to Instagram when his finger instinctively tapped on the Tinder app.

He saw he had two more matches. A brunette called Rebecca, and a blonde called Amy. He smiled and was just about to message them both with his usual opening line when he thought of April and the reason that she had been the first date he had been on in months. He had taken a break from dating, and from the opposite sex in general, for a very strong reason and now he was re-entering that world, he was aware of how careful he had to be. How easy it would be to slip back into his old ways. All the girls. All the drunken shagging. All the cheating.

And that night with Louise.

Even standing here now, filled with the optimism that came with a successful date and drowning in the brilliant sunlight of a picturesque day, he knew he would never be able to feel truly at peace with his life. He had made a mistake. He had done a bad thing. He could easily have lost everything. His job. His credibility.

His freedom.

Where was Louise now? What was she doing? Was she okay?

They were the questions that came into his mind as he stood in the middle of the bridge and looked down at the fast-flowing river that ran underneath him. But really, they weren't the questions to which he wanted answers. There was only one question that mattered because the answer could destroy his life forever.

Would she ever tell anyone what happened?

April

08:34

Borough High Street, Central London

April Adams had seen the light. All this time she had just been doing it wrong. No wonder she was still single. The drunken dates, the one-night stands, being ghosted, treating them mean to keep them keen or being keen only to end up looking like a desperate bean. Of course, none of it had worked. Because she hadn't been herself in any of those situations. She had been intoxicated, or trying something she had read in a magazine, or pretending to be the main character in her favourite rom com, (which had, for many years, been Bridget Jones).

Basically, she had been doing all the things that didn't come naturally to her, and because of that, all her previous encounters with men had resulted in her being less authentic than a Chanel handbag bought from Putney Market.

Until today.

The date with Joe had gone well. So well that they had already planned for a second one. And the best thing about it was that there had been no acting, or alcohol, or bad decisions in sight. Just clean, crisp, fun conversation over a coffee at Caffe Nero at 8 am. Who knew dating could be so simple?

She felt a wave of relief washing over her as she made her way towards her office in Borough. It was the relief that came with knowing that dating didn't have to be the awkward disaster that she had spent most of her twenties believing it to be. It didn't just have to be about swiping right as many times as you could in an hour and hoping you struck gold, a strategy which seemed about as reliable as buying a dozen lottery tickets and expecting to be an instant millionaire. It didn't have to be about waking up in a strange bed in a strange part of the city and hoping that the guy you had only just met and already slept with somehow felt like wanting to see you again for anything other than a late night booty call. And it definitely didn't have to be accompanied by the constant headache, dread and anxiety that came with being hungover and questioning whether you were destined to go through your whole life as single as the last Pringle in the tub.

It felt like a whole new world had suddenly opened up to her, and she knew who she had to thank for that.

She took out her iPhone and made a call to her best friend, Katie. She had promised to text her straight after the date, but she was so excited that a simple message wouldn't have done the job. She wanted to speak to her in person and say thank you for changing her life.

Katie answered on the second ring. She had no doubt already been holding the phone, playing that puzzle game that she loved so much. At this time of morning, she was presumably still on the bus to work.

"Hi slut" was the affectionate salutation that greeted April from the other end of the line.

April rolled her eyes, used to her friend's charming way with words by now. They had been besties since meeting at uiniversity, and besides her mother and sister, there wasn't another woman on the planet who knew her as well as Katie did.

"Alright Fleabag" April replied, using the greeting that had become customary since she had spotted Katie's resemblance to the British television character famous for her drunken, sexually explicit behaviour. The comparison applied mainly to her looks, but there was also more than a little similarity in the personality department.

Katie was just as debauched as April was, except it came more naturally to her. For April nothing came naturally. Not dating, not dieting and certainly not walking in this new pair of heels she had forced her feet into this morning.

"So, how did it go?" Katie asked over the loud hum of the bus engine she was sitting in close proximity to.

"Well, we had a coffee and we had a chat," April teased, deliberately drawing out the story to intrigue her friend even further.

"Annnnd?" Katie replied impatiently, anticipating some juicy gossip or a hilarious story following her friend's date this morning.

"And we're going to see each other again."

"Arghhhhhhhh!" Katie screamed down the phone, almost loudly enough to shatter April's eardrum.

"Calm down, it's only a second date," April said when the screaming on the other end of the line had stopped.

"Yeah but you literally never do second dates," Katie reminded her, and it was true, second dates had been a rare occurrence for her in recent times. *"See, I told you morning dating was the way to go."*

"You might be right," April said as she continued her journey to work, enjoying the warmth of the sun on her face and feeling that everything might actually be alright in the world for once.

"So, tell me everything!" Katie demanded eagerly, probably taking out a notepad and pen at the same time. "And don't leave anything out!"

April felt herself smiling again and realised she hadn't felt this good about a guy in a long time.

"Well he works in insurance," she told her friend as she stopped and waited to cross a busy street.

"Oooo money," Katie instantly retorted, and April laughed again.

"Yeah but he's not like that. He's pretty chilled, hangs out with his mates, plays football, that kind of thing."

"Are any of his mates single?" Katie asked, and April imagined her leaning forward in her bus seat in hopeful curiosity as she said it.

"Let's see how it goes with me first before we try setting you up shall we?" April told her.

"Fair enough. So when's the second date?"

"He's going to pick somewhere and let me know."

"How exciting!"

"I know."

April felt herself beaming again as she stepped off the pavement and crossed over to the other side of the street.

"Well I'd better go, I'm at the office," she said as she reached the tall grey building where she worked.

"Okay babe, text you later."

"Mwah."

April hung up, then fished her security pass out of her cluttered handbag. She tapped it on the access reader, pushed open the heavy glass door and went inside. As she made her way through reception and towards the lift, she thought about how much she had already crammed into this morning. A gym session, followed by a date with a good-looking guy. And all before breakfast.

Not bad at all.

As she stepped into the lift, she thought that maybe this was what it was like to finally be a grown-up. Instead of snoozing her alarm until the last minute or waking up with yet another hangover on a weekday morning, she had instead got up early and been super productive. Exercise, socialising and gentle strolls into work had replaced sleeping, bad eating habits and rushed tube journeys and even though it was early days, she thought this might just be the way to do it from now on. Of course, she knew that when her alarm went off tomorrow morning, all those good intentions could vanish as quickly as some of her previous dates, but this time, she felt more determined to make positive changes in her life.

The lift doors slid open, and she stepped out into the sixth-floor office rented by Five Star Designs, the boutique furniture company she had been a part of for the last two years. She rarely arrived for her 9 am start with so much time to spare, so was immediately struck by how quiet the office was. If she had wanted to, she could have continued the date with Joe for another ten minutes or so, but she had made the conscious decision to end it a little earlier by using the excuse of having to get to work. The date had been going so well that she hadn't wanted to mess it up, which she had been nervous would become more of a possibility the longer it went on. There's a reason why people say quit while you're ahead. Because it's true.

Especially when it comes to dating.

"What's the matter, did you break your bed or something?"

April jumped a little and spun around to see where the male voice had come from. She saw it was just Derek, one of the project designers, sitting at his desk in the corner.

"Sorry, what?" she asked, a little flustered.

Derek made a big show of checking the watch on his wrist and raising his eyebrows.

"I've never seen you in at this time before. I thought maybe your bed has collapsed and forced you into work early."

He seemed to find his little attempt at observational humour very amusing. A classic middle-aged dad joke. But he was more senior than her, and he had a say in the bonus she was expecting to receive in August, so she responded in the only way she could.

With excessive and exaggerated laughter.

He grinned when he saw that his joke had gone down well. While she knew that she shouldn't encourage him, she acknowledged that putting up with Derek's bad jokes was a small price to pay for a decent bonus at the end of each financial year.

"Good one," she said as she reached her desk and pulled her chair out.

"So really, what brings you in so early?" he asked, whilst watching her fiddle with the dodgy cable for her PC monitor that meant it never came on the first time of trying.

"Oh, nothing special. Just went to the gym," she replied, having made the decision not to mention the date her date with Joe.

Derek was sweet and harmless enough, but he was also a bit of a pervert, and the last thing she needed was him asking questions about her love life. It was funny how everywhere she had worked there had always been at least one person in the office who seemed to get away with making sexual innuendos. Derek was Five Star Design's designated person for all things inappropriate. April had also learnt that the more senior you were, the less likely HR were to do anything about it.

Isn't office life wonderful?

"The gym? I am impressed" Derek said, leaning back in his chair and allowing his sizeable stomach to put increasing pressure on the buttons of his tightly-fitting shirt. *"So, what were you working out today?"*

She looked back over at him and caught him eyeing her up and down, which was just another way he had of making the female employees feel uncomfortable. She had thought about turning the tables on him before by making suggestive remarks about his body while leering at him from across the room. But that would only encourage him. Besides, it was hard to make anything sound sexy about him. Forget abs of steel, his were more like abs of melted pastry. Bulging biceps? More like baggy bingo wings. To say he'd let himself go was an understatement.

He'd let himself go so much he was practically in Asia.

"Just my core" April said, trying to keep her answers as unspecific as possible. The last thing she needed to tell him was that she had spent an hour doing an Infernos Pilates class designed to target her bum and thighs. He probably would have needed hosing down with cold water if she had told him that.

"Ahhh your core," he said resting his hands on his stomach. *"So, what does that involve then?"*

April sighed and made a mental note never to get to the office this early again.

"All sorts of exercises, it's quite hard to explain," she said, then suddenly came up with an idea about how to evade any further questions. *"I'm going to make a drink; would you like one?"*
She stood up from her desk and headed for the kitchen as quickly as she could.

"I'm okay thanks. I was just wondering though..."

April could see the sanctuary of the kitchen not too far away. But she stopped, bracing herself for the next dodgy comment from Derek.

"Do you shower at the gym?"

"Excuse me?" April asked, beginning to think it might finally be time to have another conversation with HR.

"It's just I noticed that you don't have a gym bag and I was wondering where you change afterwards. But I guess you have a locker at the gym?"

April suddenly froze and looked towards her desk. There should have been a gym bag sitting on the carpet underneath her workstation. Except there wasn't. Which meant she had left it somewhere.

She retraced the morning's events in her head.

Left the gym. Walked to the tube. Got to the coffee shop. Met Joe. Walked to work.

Then she realised.

She had left her bag in the coffee shop.

Just when it seemed like her morning couldn't have gone any better, she was reminded that, as usual, nothing in her life ever went to plan.

Jazmine

08:35

Cannon Street Station, Central London

Jazmine Richards couldn't understand what all the fuss was about. She kept assuring the concerned male train station employee who was sitting beside her that she was okay and just wanted to go to work, but he insisted that she wait for somebody to come and check on her.

Somebody with knowledge of medical conditions.

Apparently, she was in shock. Okay, so she had just seen a man commit suicide by jumping in front of a train and okay, she had just heard the sound of his body smashing into the front of the carriage, but that didn't mean she needed medical attention. Surely that should be saved for the poor woman who had been driving the train and had probably been affected more than her. She'd even seen a young man on the platform be sick immediately after the awful incident, so why wasn't he in here being monitored like she was?

In here.

That was the thing. As much as she tried, Jazmine couldn't actually remember how she had ended up in this small office with an anxious member of staff peering unnervingly at her.

The room was windowless and dingy. A tatty calendar hung on the wall, still showing May despite it being June. There were messy piles of paper on the desks, most of them bearing the Transport for London logo. And there was a computer monitor on one of the desks nearby showing CCTV footage of different platforms in the station.

Her eye was quickly drawn to one of them because it was the only one where the platform was empty. A train was parked beside it, and several figures appeared to be moving around on the track in front of it.

She realised with a jolt that it was the scene of the suicide she had just witnessed.

Her guardian must have clocked her ashen face.

"Let's just turn this off, shall we?" he said, reaching sheepishly over to the monitor and pressing the power button.

The screen was suddenly black. Gone. Just like the man on the platform.

"Would you like some water?" he asked her, holding out a bottle of Evian towards her for the third time in the last two minutes.

"I'm fine, honestly," she said again, refusing the drink. *"I've told you; I really need to get to work. I've got a meeting at nine o'clock, and I have to be there."*

With that said, she went to stand up again but instead of rising to her feet and heading for the door of the office, she wobbled and felt her body slump back down into the chair.

"Just take it easy," the man in the dark blue station staff uniform told her, having thrust out his arms to steady her.

While she hadn't been particularly concerned before, now she began to worry.

Why can't I stand up?

What's happening to me?

And that nagging question again...

How did I end up in this room?

"Why am I here?" she asked the man, realising her voice was shaking as she spoke.

"You don't remember?" he replied, looking towards the door and clearly wishing somebody more qualified to handle this situation would walk through it.

The fact he had just answered a question with a question showed how much he was struggling to deal with the situation.

"No, I mean I remember waiting for my train then seeing the man next to me jump in front of it. And I found his wallet on the floor by my feet. He was called Craig Miller. There was a lot of money in the wallet. I handed it to one of the staff members. Everyone else was screaming and trying to get away, but I kept calm and did what I could. Of course, the man was clearly dead. I heard the train hit him. It was going so fast. The sound, it was like a splattering. I saw some blood. Weird really. I thought there would be more. I don't know why I thought that. Quite a strange thought to have really. But it's such a shame he felt that was the only thing he could do. If only he had talked to someone. His wife maybe? I presume he was married. I don't know, maybe not. I wonder if he had children. God, what a shame if he did. It's really awful don't you think? But I gave the wallet in, and I just wanted to get to work. I'm sure you have plenty of cameras on the tracks, and there were

dozens of other witnesses, so I don't know why you need to speak to me."

Jazmine stopped talking, suddenly realising that she had been rambling on for god knows how long and the poor guy she was talking to was just sitting there with a bemused look on his face.

That was weird. She had never been what one would call a talker. She chose her words carefully, and if she didn't have something important to say, she generally didn't say anything at all. It had served her well in her forty-eight years of life so far. As a child, when she had grown up in a household in which her parents abided by the rule that children should be seen and not heard. In her adulthood and career, where she managed a team of six PR assistants for a multi-national energy drink company by keeping communication short and succinct. And certainly in her marriage, where she had soon discovered that the less she and her husband of fourteen years conversed with each other, the better.

Yes, she was selective with her words. Yet here she was pouring them out like they were confetti.

What was wrong with her?

Instinctively, she put her hand to her mouth as if to ensure she didn't say anything else. It seemed almost as if her body's reflexes were responding to her out-of-character behaviour. The man sitting beside her could clearly see that she was a little shaken now and offered her a gentle smile.

"That's right. There was a terrible incident with the trains a short while ago. That's why you're here."

He paused for a moment and looked at the door again. He was clearly trying to decide if he should say the next thing he had in mind, so Jazmine thought it best to prompt him.

"Why don't I remember coming in here?" she asked and nodded to him as a sign that she was ready to hear his explanation.

The man sighed, tore his gaze away from the door and looked back to her. He had clearly resigned himself to the fact that help wasn't coming any time soon and that if you want a job doing, it's usually best to do it yourself.

"You were behaving a little oddly," he told her calmly.

Jazmine furrowed her brow. That didn't sound right. Behaving oddly? What did that mean? There must have been a mistake.

"What are you talking about?" she asked, aware that her pulse was increasing and that she was beginning to get flustered.

"It's okay, it was nothing too bad. Don't worry. But we thought it best to bring you in here, just while we make sure you're okay."

The man smiled and nodded again. Jazmine knew he was just trying to reassure her, but he was beginning to resemble a nodding dog.

"My colleague and I brought you in here. He's waiting outside for the paramedics. The first crew that arrived are dealing with the poor chap who jumped, but there should be somebody here to see you any minute."

She was about to interject again but paused instead, trying to recall the last thing that she could remember herself doing. She had been heading for the escalators. She had been on her way out. Yet somehow, she had ended up in here. Behaving oddly? That didn't sound good. She had to know.

"What was I doing?" she asked, almost a little fearful for the answer.

She knew how busy the Underground was. The thought of embarrassing herself in front of all those people was mortifying. Did she really want to know what she had done?

Yes, the suspense was killing her. She stared at the man, waiting for his response.

"Don't worry. It was nothing too silly, and based on what you just witnessed down on the platform, it's perfectly understandable that you would be a little shaken up."

Shaken up? Why did he keep talking to her like she was the victim in all this? Surely that was the poor guy who had met a grisly end under the wheels of a speeding train. She had merely been a bystander. She had even turned away before she saw him go under the vehicle.

But the sound. There had been no blocking that out.

"What was I doing?" she asked again, firmly enough to convince the man that he wasn't going to get away with evading her question for a second time.

"Like I said, don't worry too much but..."

"Tell me."

He took a deep breath.

"You were trying to walk up the downward escalator."

"I was what?"

"You were trying to get out. But you were using the wrong escalator. Instead of walking up the one that goes up, you were trying to walk up the one that goes down."

He giggled slightly as he finished speaking, half out of embarrassment and half because he was just trying to brush it off as something minor and make her feel better.

But there was no chance of that now. Instantly she had the image in her mind of herself on that escalator, moving one foot after the other but getting nowhere. What a sight. She must have looked ridiculous.

She felt a wave of nausea rising in her stomach. It was caused by shame. What the hell had possessed her to do such a thing?

Despite her best efforts, she was unable to prevent tears from pricking the corners of her eyes, and one small drop escaped, trickling woefully down her cheek before she had time to wipe it away.

The man sprung up off his seat and retrieved the box of tissues that was sitting beside the computer in the corner of the desk.

"Here you go" he offered kindly, giving her the box and smiling again.

Jazmine dabbed at her eyes with a tissue and screamed at herself internally to stop this nonsense. She was a strong woman. A loyal wife and a successful businesswoman. She had survived a redundancy, a car accident in her teens and two miscarriages. And she hadn't shed a single tear during any of those events. It wasn't that she was cold-hearted or emotionally stunted. It was just her way of dealing with things. Stiff upper lip. Life goes on. Crying is for other people. Not her.

So why was she blubbing away now? Why today?

"You've been through an ordeal. I know you might not think it but what you saw earlier this morning, well, not many people see things like that. Especially not when they're just on their way to work."

Of course, that's what it was Jazmine thought, as she wiped her eyes and tried to regain her composure. She had seen a man die. Right in front of her. A man who had been standing next to her. A man who hadn't tutted at her when she had accidentally bumped into him while jockeying for position as the train arrived. A man who had seemed completely normal and no different to anybody else on that platform. But he had been different.

Because he was the only one who had jumped on to the tracks.

There was a knock on the door and Jazmine jumped a little, startled by the sound in the otherwise quiet room.

"It's okay" he reassured her again, standing up to go and see who was there.

He pulled the door open and Jazmine saw one male and one female paramedic standing on the other side of it. They wore their hi-viz green uniforms, and the man had a large medi-pack slung over one of his shoulders. He looked about forty. The woman was younger, in her late twenties. They made a slightly odd team, but when they stepped inside and saw Jazmine, they both displayed the same compassionate facial expression in an attempt to reassure her that everything was going to be alright. Which of course, they were trained to do. Just like they were trained to say:

"Hi Jazmine? How are you feeling?"

"I believe it has been a bit of a tough morning."

"We're just going to check how you're doing, alright?"

"Can you tell me what day it is?"

"How many fingers am I holding up?"

"I'm going to take your temperature, okay?"

"Look straight ahead for me and try not to blink."

"Now it's perfectly natural to feel like this."

And other such things that left Jazmine feeling like the walls of the tiny office were closing rapidly in on her.

"I need some fresh air," she said before they could say anything else.

"Okay, that's a good idea. Do you need a hand getting up?"

"I'm fine," she snapped back, her embarrassment making way for her familiar streak of defiance.

But then she stood up and realised that she did need a hand if she were to avoid falling back into the seat.

The paramedics escorted Jazmine out of the office and thanked the station employee for his help as they left. As the three of them made their way through the ticket hall towards the barriers that led to the daylight of a London morning, Jazmine noticed how crowded the area was. Hundreds of frustrated commuters were either trying to get through the barrier towards the platforms or were giving up and heading back outside.

As the paramedics carefully guided her through the crowd, she heard a female voice over the tannoy system providing an update on the situation.

"There are currently severe delays on the District Line due to a person on the tracks here at Cannon Street. If you can, we advise you seek alternative routes. Thank you."

Jazmine heard several loud groans from the people she was passing through, but it was the voice of a disgruntled man that struck her.

"Why couldn't the selfish bugger just kill themself at home and save us all the hassle."

Before she really knew what she was doing, she had pulled away from the paramedics, turned back towards the man who had said it and looked him square in the eye with an uncontrollable rage coursing through her.

The man instantly froze, unsure what was about to happen.

"He wasn't selfish. He was just a normal person" she said. *"He was just like you or me. He was just going to work. Until he couldn't do it anymore. His name was Craig Miller. Respect him!"*

Jazmine was going to continue her outburst until she felt the hand of the female paramedic on her arm. She turned around and realised that everyone was staring at her.

"Come on, let's go and get that fresh air," the paramedic said gently and, to Jazmine, that sounded like the best idea in the world.

Keith

08:36

Tower Bridge, Central London

Keith Jones checked his watch again, but it only confirmed what he already suspected. The meeting had been scheduled to start six minutes ago, and there was still one person missing. It was now starting to dawn on him that despite his best intentions, Craig Miller wasn't going to show up today.

It made perfect sense.

Why would he show up after I warned him? What did he have to gain from being here to face the music?

But another question was taking hold in Keith's mind, and it was one to which he was afraid to know the answer.

If Craig isn't here because he knows how bad it is, then where is he?

Keith was beginning to regret tipping off his friend and colleague about the fact that his fraudulent insurance scams had been rumbled and that the police were going to be involved. Using a phone box, for obvious reasons, he had called Craig the previous morning, believing at the time that he was doing a good thing. He was giving Craig a twenty-four-hour head start before his imminent arrest, allowing him the opportunity to get his affairs in order, as well as to avoid being blindsided at work the next day. But now he realised how naïve he had been.

Perhaps instead of hanging up the phone and trying to get his story straight before the questions began, Craig had thrown what he could into a suitcase and fled. He could be anywhere by now. One thing was for sure. He wasn't sitting at the boardroom table on the 22nd floor of the offices of Barringdon Insurers, where he should have been.

Keith was in attendance in his role as Head of Compliance, a position he had held for just over nine years. Being sixty-one, he had planned for this to be his last job before retirement anyway, but now he was almost certain that it would be. The chances of being employed in a similar role anywhere else in the future after it came out that someone in his office had been forging signatures were slim to none. In fact, when the investigations into the fraud were eventually over, he would do well to avoid losing the job he currently had.

Sitting beside him was Cath Simpson, their fifty-three-year-old HR manager. Her pen was poised over her notebook, but she displayed none of her usual bubbliness or enthusiasm for work. She was close to Craig, and the bombshell of what he had been up to under all their noses had hit her particularly hard. But despite her affection for him, she was a true professional, and there had been no danger of her tipping Craig off since the discovery of his deeds on Friday afternoon. Only Keith had been stupid enough to do that.

Across the table from them was Matt Ryan, the forty-eight-year-old Director of the company and a man who had always seemed to ooze self-confidence and control. But today he was just as quiet and pensive as them all. Like Keith, he would have some very difficult questions to answer from the other Board members, and because it had been his signature that Craig had forged numerous times as part of his scam, he might even face some uncomfortable enquiries from the police. But Matt was an honest bloke, and it was clear to anyone who knew him that he had been kept in the dark just as much as every one of the 1,500 employees in the London branch of one of the largest and most successful insurance companies in the UK.

And finally, beside Matt, was the empty chair that was supposed to belong to Craig. He should have walked in here at 08:30 in his typically flamboyant manner, waxing lyrical about something he had done over the weekend and how much business he was going to bring in that coming week. He should have flirted harmlessly with Cath, slapped Matt on the back and winked at Keith, before taking his seat and opening up his notebook. And he should have sat there as he was informed that he had been invited to this meeting not to discuss company business but to be told that he was suspended pending a criminal investigation because they had uncovered evidence of multiple counts of insurance fraud linking back to him.

But none of those things had happened because Craig wasn't here yet.

"Maybe there's a problem with the trains" Cath suggested, likely more out of an attempt to cut the silence in the room than because it was something she actually believed.

Keith saw Matt check the time on his company mobile and shake his head again. He wasn't buying it. Keith began to worry that if Craig was a no-show, then fingers might start to be pointed at him because the truth was that only three people in the company were supposed to know the real reason for this meeting today.

The first was Matt, who had discovered Craig's illegal forgeries when he had been asked to look back over historic insurance settlements and realised that he didn't remember agreeing to pay out on certain ones that had been signed off in his name. Secondly, there was Keith, who had been drafted in by Matt to look through the forgeries, only to uncover a whole mountain of incriminating evidence ultimately linking back to Craig. And finally, Cath, who had been consulted on the next steps to take from a Human Resources point of view. So if Craig didn't appear in the office today and it turned out he had fled, Matt would have no choice but to suspect either Keith or Cath as being the informer.

As scary as that was, a glimmer of hope crept slowly into Keith's mind as he guiltily considered the most likely outcome. Based on their respective relationships with the suspected criminal, Matt was more likely to suspect Cath of breaking the veil of secrecy, leaving Keith to escape punishment. Cath and Craig had a great rapport. They worked late together. They ran staff functions together. They were always the last two drinking at the bar together at Christmas parties. Some of their colleagues had even suspected them of having a sexual relationship, although it had never been proven and Keith certainly thought that it seemed unlikely. Cath was a bit too old for Craig. He liked his woman younger than her.

As in, thirty years younger.

In comparison, Keith and Craig were merely colleagues, and their relationship was purely professional. At least that was how it appeared to the untrained eye. In reality, the pair were bonded more closely than anybody could imagine, because of what had happened at an infamous staff party seven years earlier.

It had been a crisp autumn evening in October 2013 when all the employees of Barringdon had gathered at the Dorchester Hotel in Mayfair for their annual in-house awards ceremony. The dress code had been black tie for the men and ballgowns for the women, and Keith had been feeling particularly dapper that night in his rented tuxedo. He had also been feeling unencumbered because his wife of twenty-six years, Madeline, had been unable to attend alongside him after succumbing to a bout of flu. She had insisted that he attend without her, however, and he had been grateful for that, mostly because he didn't get out much anymore and often relied on work events to fill in the large gaps that were emerging in his social life as he grew older.

He had taken his seat that evening on the table reserved for the management team. Cath and her now ex-husband had been there, as had Matt and his wife, alongside several other VIP's. And lastly, there had been Craig, ever the networker, who had taken the opportunity to leave his table with the sales team and jump into the seat that was going spare after Keith's wife had given up hers.

The conversation, humour and red wine had flowed throughout the meal. The awards had been handed out by the hilarious celebrity compere. And Keith had been having a grand old time with everybody in attendance. So much so that by the time the tables were cleared away and the guests had moved into the adjacent room where the DJ and dancefloor were waiting, he was beginning to feel like he'd overdone it slightly. A quick trip to the bathroom had shown him that his chubby face was bright red and that his bowtie was now undone and hanging loose around his neck. But instead of quitting while he was ahead and retiring to his hotel room to sleep it off, he had headed back onto the dancefloor via another visit to the bar.

It was on the dancefloor that he had got talking to Isabella, the forty-year-old Portuguese woman who was part of the cleaning team that serviced their offices on a daily basis. Matt had been the one to suggest inviting the cleaners to the event; he had argued that if it weren't for them, the offices wouldn't be fit for purpose, but Keith suspected that he had an ulterior motive. Matt had, at the time, been playing a single-minded game that would eventually gain him a promotion to Director, and his magnanimous approach to the party had surely just been another strategic move to demonstrate his credentials as a really decent guy as well as a business-minded one.

But with hindsight, Keith would wish the cleaners had not been there that evening. Or at least that Isabella hadn't been. The drunker she had got, the more she had flirted with the older and, in her eyes, powerful Head of Compliance. And the drunker he had got, the more he had flirted in return with the younger, attractive Portuguese cleaner. By the time the music had stopped, and the guests had begun drifting upstairs to their respective rooms, Keith and Isabella had formed quite the bond.

It was a bond that had resulted in him accepting her offer to finish the last of their drinks in her room, on the twelfth floor and ultimately, in his inebriated and misguided state, he had ended up in bed with a woman who was not his wife. By the time he had woken up after passing out, the daylight had been streaming through the windows, and he was facing the consequences of his actions in his sober, sorrowful state.

He had left the room as quickly as he could in a haze of confusion and regret, only to bump into another colleague as he closed the door on his shameful little secret. Craig had been passing by at that exact moment and had seen Keith stumbling out into the corridor looking mortified at what he had just done, and despite trying to cover it up, his younger colleague knew something interesting and deceitful had just happened.

Keith, with Craig in tow, had made his way miserably up to the room on the fifteenth floor where he should have slept. He had sunk onto the bed, head in hands, and admitted to his young colleague how mortified he was that he had cheated on his wife and how worried he was that his marriage would be over if the cleaner were to gossip. To his surprise, Craig, after much laughter and back slapping, had promised Keith that that would not happen and, to be fair, he had been right.

To this day, Keith didn't know the full story of what went down after that conversation with Craig. All he knew was that Isabella left her job with the cleaning company that very week and was never seen again, and when asked what happened, Craig merely winked and said he was an expert in paying women to do what he wanted. Clearly, Craig had paid off Isabella so she wouldn't be around the office anymore, and although Keith hadn't fully understood why he had done this for him, he had nonetheless been extremely grateful. His wife had never found out what happened that night seven years ago, so needless to say, he had felt indebted to Craig ever since.

It wasn't until Friday afternoon, just three days ago, that he had finally figured out what Craig had been paying for when he had given Isabella that money. He hadn't been paying it as a favour to his stupid work friend who had been worried about his marriage. He had been paying it to gain the debt of his stupid work friend who worked in a powerful department. A department that he would need good favour with when it came to running his scam.

Compliance.

Keith had not been complicit in any of the illegal activity Craig had been involved in, but when he thought back over the last couple of years, he recognised that he had certainly not done enough to look into the work that Craig had passed over his desk. Essentially, he felt like he owed the man who had saved his marriage, so had often bent the rules for him and been less rigorous when checking Craig's documents than he was when checking those of every other employee. He had always given Craig the benefit of the doubt and by doing so had missed multiple opportunities to spot the fraudulent behaviour sooner. It had only been when somebody in his team had flagged it up on Friday that he had discovered the real damage that his stupid act of infidelity had caused. Craig had been using him and however much money he had given to Isabella to make her leave all those years ago, it almost certainly paled in comparison to the amount of money Craig had been swindling from the company for the last few years.

"Something's wrong," Matt said, shattering the silence that had dominated the room and causing Keith to snap out of his worries. *"He's never been late for a meeting in all the time I've known him. Even with all the hangovers."*

Keith and Cath shared a concerned look.

"I think we should give him a few more minutes," Keith suggested, trying to buy time even though he was now certain Craig was probably already in a different country using his ill-gotten gains to start up a new and secretive life. *"Cath's right. There's probably a problem with the trains."*

Matt stared at Keith and, for a second, the older man thought he was going to be accused of tipping Craig off after all. But then the Director just threw up his hands and conceded.

"Fine, five more minutes. Then I'm calling the police," he said, sitting back and folding his arms across his suit.

Keith swallowed hard, aware that once the police were involved, things would never be the same at Barringdon again. There would be inquests, finger-pointing and job losses, but it would be nothing compared to what Craig was facing. Keith felt sick to his stomach about how things had turned out.

But then there was a knock on the door that made them all jump.

Keith, Matt and Cath instantly bolted up from their chairs and stared in the direction of the sound. Maybe he had turned up after all. Maybe he was here.

Maybe it was Craig.

But then the door opened and Mohammed, a sales rep from Craig's team, poked his head sheepishly inside.

"S-s-sorry to interrupt," he stammered. *"But reception keeps calling, and I don't know what to do."*

"What is it?" Matt growled, revealing every part of the stress he had been bearing over the last few days.

"Erm," Mohammed offered, struggling to speak in front of such senior members of staff. *"They say there's a young schoolboy in reception and he's asking to speak to Craig."*

"He's not the only one that wants to speak to him," Matt grumbled back, turning away from the door.

He was just about to take his seat again when Mohammed continued.

"I know that Sir, but he says he's Craig's son."

Harry

08:37

Tower Bridge, Central London

Harry Baxter continued to fidget with the handles on his school rucksack as he sat in the reception area of Barringdon Insurers and tried not to look too out of place. But it was a difficult task. After all, he was clearly the only twelve-year-old here, and his school uniform certainly wasn't helping him to blend in. Everyone else was much older, much more smartly dressed and more obviously suited to being here. They all had appointments or meetings and somebody to come down and greet them on arrival. But Harry didn't have any of that. He just kept getting puzzled looks from people as they walked past. Even the woman sitting behind the big desk with all the telephones looked confused.

This grown-up world was weird Harry thought as he took another deep breath and looked back at his rucksack.

In the middle of a crowded, noisy city, he had never felt more alone.

It had already been a bit of an ordeal just to get here, and his body was a jumbled mess of emotions. He felt guilty for lying to his mother about walking to school earlier when he had actually snuck off and caught a train into London. He felt stressed, having navigated the Underground system alone for the first time, especially since he had been forced to get off his train early because somebody had fallen on the tracks up ahead. And now he was simply worried that he had made a mistake coming here, that his dad wouldn't want to see him, and that he would end up getting in trouble for nothing.

But most of all, he felt sad. That was because he just wanted to meet his father for the first time and now that he was here, in the building where he worked, it should be an exciting time for him. But it suddenly didn't seem exciting. It seemed scary.

Not because his dad might walk into the reception area and see Harry.

But because he might not want to.

Harry looked back at the blonde-haired woman sitting behind the large white desk across the room from him. She looked about the same age as his mum, which was twenty-nine, but she wore a lot more makeup than his mum did. She also dressed a lot differently, wearing a tight black dress and sharp heels, which were really different to the hoodies and jogging bottoms his mum spent most of her time in. But then his mum worked from home, while this woman seemed to have a much more important job. She seemed to be in charge of this whole building, deciding who got to go up in the lifts and who had to sit and wait in the reception. Sometimes she would wave at the person walking through the revolving glass doors and smile as they passed her, but sometimes she would make the person sign their name and take a seat on one of the blue sofas, which was what she had done to him.

Instead of a wave and a smile, he had had to write out his name and the person he was visiting today. So that's what he had done.

Name: **Harry Baxter**

Visiting: **Craig (my dad)**

When he had given the piece of paper to the receptionist, she had frowned and asked him if he had a surname for Craig. He had nodded enthusiastically and said that it was Miller.

"Craig Miller?" she had asked him. *"Are you sure?"*

He had confirmed that he was. Of course he was. He had spent hours poring over every detail of this man on LinkedIn, ever since his mum's friend had spotted Craig drinking in a bar and sent a photo to his mum, which Harry had intercepted and matched to his online profile.

He knew it had been a lucky find to spot him on LinkedIn which Harry had figured out seemed to be some kind of boring website for grown-ups who had jobs. Not at all as exciting as YouTube or TikTok. But he had googled his father's name, and while searching through the many results, he had eventually found the photo that matched the one that he had stolen from his mum's phone. From there he had been able to find the name of the company he worked at, and now here he was sitting in the same building as the man he had never met before. But he couldn't understand why the receptionist had seemed so confused about it all. He was a child, and he had figured out where his father was.

She was a grown-up, so why did she keep looking at him with that weird expression on her face?

After a few minutes of her asking him if he was really sure he was in the right place and him nodding and saying that he was, she had eventually asked him to take a seat on one of the sofas while she tried to find out where Craig was. She said she wasn't sure if he was in the office yet, but that he might have come in before she started work so she would have to try and find out. Harry had rushed excitedly rushed over to the sofa, where he had unloaded the heavy rucksack from his shoulders and taken a seat. Because she didn't know whether his dad was already here or not meant Harry had spent the last fifteen minutes checking between the revolving entrance doors and the sliding lift doors for any sign of him. But so far, there had been none.

Harry started to worry that this meant that his dad didn't want to meet him for the first time, but he was also aware he was in the adult world now and that there might be another reason for him not being here yet. Like maybe he was so busy working that he hadn't had time to come downstairs yet. Or maybe, like Harry, he had been stuck on the trains and been forced to get off at a different station and walk. There could be many reasons why he wasn't here yet.

Just then, another possible reason popped into Harry's mind that he hadn't considered before. Maybe his dad hadn't come to see him yet because, just like the young boy he had fathered, he was nervous. That made perfect sense, and Harry felt a wave of optimism coursing through him. He knew how difficult it had been for him to come here today and even with the man's name, photo and place of work it had still taken him three weeks to pluck up the courage to do something about it. Perhaps his dad was going through the same nervous emotions right now somewhere in this building, worried about what might happen, worried his son might not love him. But of course, Harry would love him. He didn't care what had happened between him and his mum. He just wanted to have both of them in his life.

A phone rang loudly and made Harry jump a little in his seat. The receptionist quickly answered it; he couldn't hear what she was saying, but then he saw her looking at him, and he knew it must be something to do with him.

Was that his dad on the other end of the call? Was he here? Was he coming?

The tension was driving him mad, and when he looked down at his rucksack, he noticed he had made a tangled mess of the straps. It would be quite a job to get them undone, but at least it would take his mind off the waiting. He was just about to make a start unwrapping them when...

"Excuse me, Mr Baxter?"

Harry looked up and saw the receptionist standing over him, holding out a plastic cup of water. Being so close to her now, Harry could see exactly how much red lipstick she had on and that for some weird reason the colour of her face didn't seem to match the colour of her neck. It was like her neck was white, but her face was a little orange. Like she'd been in the sun but also got muddy at the same time. He didn't really know why she looked like that. Maybe she was ill.

"Mr Baxter?"

Harry realised he was just staring at her, still trying to figure out the different shades of colour on her upper body.

"I'm sorry," she said, smiling and showing off a set of perfect white teeth. *"There's me still in business mode. I'll call you Harry, how about that?"*

Harry couldn't help but smile back. This woman was nothing like the women he was used to seeing in his normal life. His mum didn't look like this. His teachers didn't look like this. And none of the girls in his class looked like this.

Why couldn't he see more women like her around?

He was still staring at her when she moved the cup of water closer towards him.

"I thought you might like a drink of water while you wait."

He reluctantly moved his eyes down from her smiling face and looked at the clear plastic cup she was trying to give him. He realised that he was actually quite thirsty now, so took the cup from her, only to spill half of it down himself in the process.

"Oh, I'm sorry, would you like a tissue?" she asked, clearly concerned, but in a way that made Harry feel very aware of being just a small boy in a school uniform.

"I'm okay," he said quickly, trying to be cool.

"Good boy," she said kindly, and Harry was entranced by the sound of her heels echoing around the cavernous reception hall as she walked back to her desk.

It felt like he had stepped into a whole new world since he had diverted from his usual path to school and begun his journey into the city centre. Ever since he had climbed up the steps at Aldgate East Station and stepped out onto the busy pavement in the bright sunshine, it had been one big adventure. First of all, he had been completely lost and confused because he had been forced to get off one stop earlier than he had planned because somebody was on the tracks ahead of the train. According to a man in Harry's carriage, that meant somebody had died. He hadn't been able to see anything, but he would definitely be telling his best friend, Mustaf, about it when he saw him at school tomorrow.

If it hadn't been for his new mobile phone, he wouldn't have known which way to go, but luckily he was able to type the address into Google Maps, and it gave him a direct line to follow. It had taken him about fifteen minutes to get there, and he had seen all sorts of things on the way. Tall buildings that went up as far as he could see. A smelly man sitting on the street shouting at everybody who walked past him. And so many angry grown-ups, all rushing around and pushing each other so much that it had been hard to avoid getting bumped into himself.

But ever since he had got into this building things had been better. It was quieter here, and everything was clean and shiny. There was the nice woman sitting at the desk, and there were many people to watch as they walked past him and disappeared inside the lifts.

Harry noticed how all the men seemed to be wearing similar clothes to him. Jacket, trousers, tie. Like a school uniform for grown-ups. He didn't know why, because his mum had promised him that when he left school, he wouldn't have to wear those things anymore. It seemed to him that she must have been lying because everybody here was wearing them. He wondered if his dad was wearing a uniform too, just like him. He hoped not. He hoped that his dad was too cool for that.

A gentle whirring sound alerted Harry to the fact that another lift had arrived on the ground floor, so he carefully watched the several silver doors in case his dad should walk out of one of them. The seconds seemed to slow down as he waited, and he realised that he was holding his breath. Finally, the doors of the second lift on the right slid open, and a man stepped out onto the marble floor.

But it wasn't his dad.

Harry felt disappointed all over again. Instead of the first glimpse of his father that he had been hoping for, he watched as an old man in a dark suit slowly made his way over to the sofa where he was sitting. The man had some grey hair but also some bald parts. He was a bit fat. Harry wondered how old he was. Seventy? Eighty? Ninety? Probably not that old, but to Harry, he looked ancient. And now the man was standing right in front of him.

"Hello, Harry is it?" he asked nervously.

Harry nodded his head and noticed the receptionist watching him again.

The old man smiled and took a seat beside him, groaning a little as he did.

"Well it's very nice to meet you, Harry," the man said, holding out a wrinkled hand towards him. *"My name is Keith."*

Harry stared at the old hand. He saw there was a gold ring on one of the fingers and also that the skin looked different to his own. It was all wrinkly.

"Is my dad coming?" Harry asked, deciding not to shake the hand because he didn't know who this man was, and his mum had always told him to be careful around strangers.

"Who is your dad?" the man asked him, slowly taking back his hand and resting it on his knee.

"Craig Miller," Harry replied excitedly. *"Do you know him?"*

Keith smiled and said *"Yes I know him. We work together."*

"Wow, what's he like?" Harry found himself asking before he had really thought about what he wanted to say.

Keith looked confused. *"What do you mean?"* he asked, glancing across at the woman on reception who was still staring at them both.

"I haven't met him before. Today is the first day I'll see him," Harry told him, feeling excited to be telling someone this but then a little disappointed that the old man didn't seem to be as excited about it as he was.

"You've never met your father before?" the man asked, and Harry shook his head vigorously.

"Oh," the man said, scratching his wrinkled face as the phone on reception rang again.

He was just about to speak to Harry again when the woman called out to him.

"What is it?" he asked in a grumpy voice, and Harry knew the man must be annoyed because he sounded just like his mum did when he was bugging her about something.

"It's the police," the woman said.

"The police?" Keith said, suddenly rising from the sofa and tucking in his white shirt.

The old man told him to wait there, but Harry followed sneakily behind him to the front desk. He heard the woman say something about there having been an incident on a train and that the police are trying to contact Craig's next of kin. *Whatever that meant*. Then Harry noticed how upset Keith looked as he listened on the phone, and when he finally noticed that the boy was standing behind him, Harry was surprised that he didn't shout at him. He just stared down at him and looked really sad about things.

Valentin

08:38

Canary Wharf, East London

Valentin Morozov was ready to make some money, and he had almost everything that he needed to do so. He was in position at his corner desk on the forty-third floor of the high-rise office owned by Global Sphere Investments. He had the large funds that his wealthy clients had entrusted him with at his fingertips. And most importantly, he had the sharp mind that was the key to it all and had served him well ever since he had come into the world on a freezing cold day in Russia in 1990.

The only thing he didn't have at that moment was a tool that would drown out the banal chatting from his colleagues sitting around him in the open-plan space.

Without wanting to waste another second, he reached into the inside pocket of the £2000 Armani suit jacket hanging on the back of his chair and pulled out the AirPod Pro headphones that were nestled there. They were the latest in wireless headphone technology, famed for their noise-cancelling capabilities and had cost him over £200 when he had ordered them online a couple of months earlier. He had then been concerned about losing one, so he had ordered another three pairs just to be safe.

He popped a pod into each ear and opened the Podcast App on his iPhone XR, feeling the now-familiar tingling of anticipation as he did so. Listening to the podcasts had started as a way for him to drown out the irritating voices around him, and he had spent months listening to shows related to his line of work. Podcasts with names like *Capital Gains*, *Market Edge* and *Invest Intel*, which had all been reasonably informative but pretty dry in their content. It wasn't as if he needed any of them to be successful in his job. And they sure as hell weren't the cause of his anticipation right now.

That feeling was down to the podcasts that he had unintentionally discovered one day but which had since gone on to change his life.

True crime podcasts.

These podcasts had much more exciting titles than the ones he had been used to. Titles like *From The Blood Files*, *Dark and Disturbed*, *The Monsters Amongst Us*, and of course his favourite, *I Killed Her Slowly.* If it wasn't clear from the titles, these shows were about one thing and one thing only.

Serial Killers.

Ever since he had inadvertently stumbled across this world of seemingly endless content on murders and motives, he had been consumed by it and had spent almost every possible moment listening to as much of it as he could. He had learned a lot in that time. What drives people to kill. What they do to their victims. And what causes them to get caught.

But more than that, he had learned a lot about himself. He had learned that he was turned on by these stories. He was excited by these stories. And most of all, he wanted to be one of these stories.

He had come to the decision that murder was the missing ingredient in his life and the one thing he needed to spice up his rich, comfortable but ultimately boring existence. While he hadn't yet killed anyone, he had no doubt he was capable of such an act and felt emboldened by the amount of information he had amassed from months of listening to the podcasts about the murderers who had gone before him. Plus, he had already identified his first victim. It was the auburn-haired girl who caught the same train as him from Greenwich every morning and whose mere existence was a constant source of irritation to him.

He had seen her again this morning, texting away endlessly on her phone and pouting and posing like somebody was watching. Which they were. But unlike all the other men who couldn't seem to tear their eyes away from her, Valentin didn't harbour any feelings of sexual desire for the young woman. He had a lust yes. But it was a lust for blood.

Her blood.

She was to be the starting point in his second career.

His serial killer career.

At the age of thirty, he had already mastered his first career, so he had full confidence that he would be able to master this new one. But it was impossible to be a serial killer with only one victim, so he knew it was imperative that he got away with his first murder so he would be free to build up his numbers.

The more numbers he got, the more likely he was to have whole episodes of true crime podcasts dedicated to his story.

He scrolled through the list of podcasts he subscribed to, checking for the ones that automatically downloaded new episodes to his phone upon their release. As it was only Monday, this week's episode of *I Killed Her Slowly* wasn't out yet, but he had plenty to keep him occupied until its release tomorrow.

He noticed the familiar blood-red icon for the Australian podcast *Serial 101* and read the description of today's episode.

Queensland is known as Australia's 'Sunshine State', but in 2012, the gruesome discovery of three bodies showed a much darker side to the region and led to the hunt and capture of a man who would become known as the Butcher of Bundaberg.

Perfect. That sounded like just the thing he needed to drown out the irritating sounds of office life. Eagerly, he pressed PLAY.

As he read an email from one of his most important clients, a Saudi businessman with a net worth of over £100 million, he heard the recognisable theme tune playing in his ears and the sound of the Australian narrator beginning to speak.

"The Bruce Highway is a famous stretch of road and the biggest traffic carrier in Queensland. Running from Brisbane in the south of the State all the way up to Cairns in the north, it passes through many famous cities on the East Coast including Rockhampton,

Maryborough and Mackay. The route is popular with truckers, but it's also commonly used by backpackers taking advantage of its sprawling route to traverse and take in the Sunshine State. But in 2012 the highway became known for something other than being a major transport connection when several backpackers went missing along its corridor. This is the story of the Butcher of Bundaberg."

Valentin settled into his seat and typed an email reply to the Saudi, who had informed him that he was depositing another £5 million of his wealth with the Russian, based on the excellent returns the investor had already generated for him.

"Emily Hart was a twenty-three-year-old British backpacker who had travelled from her home country alone, looking to enjoy the many attractions of Australia during her stay on a twelve-month working holiday visa. After arriving in Sydney, she spent three weeks taking in the sights and getting to know her fellow travellers in the hostel she stayed in on George Street, in the inner city. From there she decided to travel up the coast into Queensland, in search of seasonal fruit-picking work and boarded a bus to Brisbane with an American friend she had made in the hostel. From Brisbane, they headed further up the coast to Childers, a rural town in a region famous for the many varieties of fruit that grow there. The town is also known in Australia for being the scene of a tragic hostel fire that saw fifteen backpackers perish in June 2000. Emily and her friend Morgan arrived in Childers on April fourth 2012 and checked into the OrangeBowl Hostel where they put their names

down for any upcoming work at the farms that surrounded the area."

Valentin glanced at the current price of Critch Steel on one of his computer monitors, whilst accessing the fund of a Brazilian businessman and making the necessary preparations to purchase two hundred shares in Trinity Power, a company that he believed was going to be the biggest player in the renewable gas market in the coming months.

"Unfortunately, their arrival in Childers coincided with a particularly bad spell of weather in the region, which meant all fruit-picking work was suspended for several days. To pass the time, Emily and Morgan accompanied several of the other backpackers at the hostel to the town pub, where they spent a night drinking and dancing on the evening of sixth April. At around eleven pm, Emily told Morgan she was stepping outside for a cigarette but would be back shortly to buy the next round of drinks. That would be the last time Morgan saw her friend.

Two days later, while Morgan and the hostel owner were still trying to contact Emily, Faye Green, a twenty-one-year-old German backpacker from the industrial city of Dusseldorf, arrived in Bundaberg, a city fifty kilometres north of Childers, to begin work as an au pair for a young Australian family. Before beginning work at the home of the Smith family, she spent an afternoon exploring the small city, and she was seen buying items of clothing in a charity shop and enjoying an ice cream on Bourbong Street. But Faye failed to arrive at the home of the Smiths, and when they were unable to gain contact with her, they assumed she had simply had second thoughts and moved on to seek alternative work elsewhere.

It was only when the disappearance of Emily in Childers made the local news three days later that Peter Smith felt compelled to report the case of the missing German girl to the Bundaberg Police. But due to the nomadic lifestyle for which backpackers are known, the authorities didn't deem either subject to warrant further investigation at the time, simply believing that the girls had continued their travels in a different part of the country."

Valentin completed several more trades, including taking a large position with GredNeft, the fast-growing oil company that had recently taken over control of the East Siberian pipeline.

"Ten days after Peter Smith's report, Manuela Amblard, a nineteen-year-old French woman checked out of the OzLife Backpacker hostel in Rockhampton and told her friends there that she was planning to hitchhike south to Maryborough, where she believed there would be more fruit-picking jobs available. While her friends told her to take the bus, Manuela believed Australia to be safe, and she was known for having used hitchhiking to get around the country before. At around 10:40 am on the nineteenth April, a trucker from Brisbane recalled seeing a woman matching Manuela's description by the side of the Bruce Highway just outside of Rockhampton. But nobody saw or heard from Manuela again after that day, and when her family reported her missing after being unable to make contact with her, the media in Queensland picked up on the fact that three young

females had all gone missing within days of each other and all from towns located along the Bruce Highway."

Valentin read through another email and felt himself growing restless, impatient for the narrator of the podcast to get to the good part. The part with the blood and the bodies.

"The authorities in Queensland appealed for information from the public in their search for the three missing women and the police chief in charge of the investigation, Detective Nick Dangerfield, said they couldn't be sure the missing persons were connected due to the distances involved in their last-known locations but that they were keeping an open mind.

Six weeks passed by, and the media coverage began to quieten down as the investigation seemed to be leading nowhere. That was until the afternoon of Sunday eleventh June when Mick Riewoldt, a Childers resident, made the forty-five-minute drive to Bundaberg to visit his sister and her family. Only five minutes outside the city, Mick blew out a tyre on his Ute and was forced off the highway. He left his vehicle and, as he didn't have a spare tyre with him, he retreated down the banks of the roadside to a safe position, where he attempted to call for assistance. It was while making the call that he looked to his right into the dense bush that lined the busy route and saw what appeared to be a human hand, poking out from beneath several branches. He quickly called the police, and when they arrived, they soon discovered that they were dealing with a major crime scene. Three badly decomposing bodies were discovered hidden in the bush and, while it was a difficult task, they were eventually identified by their items of clothing. It was confirmed that the bodies belonged to the three missing women. Emily Hart, Faye Green and Manuela Amblard. Unfortunately, their bodies were so badly decomposed that it was impossible to establish a cause of death, but the police and the women's families would soon have their answers."

Valentin took a long refreshing sip of his ice-cold water and stretched his arms above his head before typing out a response to one of his most important clients, a Qatari Sheikh with many business interests in London. He had good news to report. He had made the Sheikh millions of pounds of profits this year and had just discovered a way to increase that figure further, thanks to an opportunity he had spotted in the futures market in New York.

"The discovery of the bodies made international news, and the hunt was on for what the police in Bundaberg described as a vicious and cold-blooded serial killer. The investigation was flooded with information from the public, but none of it turned out to be of interest until a twenty-one-year-old man came forward. Josh Stevens, a resident of Bundaberg, told police how he had been drinking in the Bundy Tavern one evening at the end of May when he had gotten into a conversation with a drunk stranger at the bar. They had discussed the missing women, and when Josh had said it reminded him of the case of Ivan Milat, the notorious Australian serial killer who had targeted backpackers in New South Wales in the late eighties and early nineties, the man had scoffed and said this was much better. He had then gone on to say that by the time this killer was done, he would make the Ivan Milat

murders look like child's play. After checking the CCTV from the tavern, the police put out a nationwide call for information on the man in the footage. Within hours, a woman by the name of Mary Jackson had come forward and admitted to the police that the man in question was her son, David."

Valentin rolled his eyes. The poor guy had been given up by his mum.

"The police were able to track down David to a motel just outside of Rockhampton, and when they got into his room, they found his body in the bathtub, where he had committed suicide while surrounded by several possessions belonging to the women he had murdered. A letter was found beside the body. In it, David had confessed to the crimes, saying he was driven to kill after being spurned numerous times over the years by female backpackers until he could take no more and decided to get revenge on the women that came to his country only to reject him. He had befriended the woman, and once they were close, he had strangled them, put them into the back of his truck and dumped their bodies by the highway outside his home city. The Butcher of Bundaberg was no more."

Valentin sent the email to his Qatari client and paused the podcast. There were still ten minutes remaining, but he had got the gist of it. It was one of the tamer episodes he had listened to, and he would make sure he found a much darker one next. But before he did that, he opened a spreadsheet on one of his monitors and looked at the three columns on the page.

P - 31

K - 67

L - 62

P stood for Police, K for Killer and L for Luck. Each figure represented the total number of cases that had been solved in that way from the podcasts that he had listened to. He added another 1 to the L column. After all, it had been luck that the man's tyre had burst at the exact spot on the huge highway where the bodies were buried. He could see from his research that in the majority of the cases of a serial killer's crimes being solved, it was either a mistake on the killer's part or sheer luck that resulted in their capture. For all their efforts, it was the police investigators that were bringing up the rear.

Valentin allowed himself to sit back in his chair for a moment and think ahead to the future, pondering which column his crimes would be slotted into. But he had a fairly good idea. The police wouldn't catch him. And he wouldn't make a mistake. Once he started to kill, the only way he would be stopped was by luck.

He could feel the anticipation building within him again. He couldn't wait to get to his first victim. The girl on his train. The girl that got on at Greenwich and got off at Herons Quays. The one with the summer dress and the auburn hair.

The girl that would soon be dead.

Olivia

08:39

Herons Quays, East London

Olivia Harringay fiddled with the strap on her summer dress and flicked back her auburn hair. She was ready for another week of work, and this one promised to be bigger than any that had gone before it. By Friday afternoon, she should have learned if she had been successful in gaining the promotion she had applied for. Five days away from more money, more power and more opportunities. Senior Editor at AMI Music, the largest online music blog in the UK and one of the top 10 in the world.

That was the goal, and she was so close to it that she could almost reach out and touch it.

But for now, she would have to make do with reaching out and turning on her desktop monitor and beginning what she hoped would be her final week as just an Editor. It would be weird to have the Senior tag before her job title, she had thought on many occasions while pondering her potential promotion. After all, she was only twenty-nine. There was nothing senior about that part of her. But in terms of experience, she fitted the bill.

As she waited for her computer to load up, she looked around the busy office and felt pride at how far she had come. It had all started when, at sixteen, she had begun writing a personal blog about her favourite musicians, and now here she was, employed by an international company, and with the power to make or break musicians by writing one simple article.

Quite an impressive leap, she thought, contentedly.

She had always been a massive music fan. As a young girl in the nineties, she had worshipped boy bands like Take That and East 17. She had even gone to bed every night as a ten-year-old with a poster of Robbie Williams above her bed. But her favourite group had always been the Spice Girls. She had listened to their CDs on repeat for hours on end, performed all the routines in the mirror while singing into her hairbrush and had even persuaded her mum to buy her a Union Jack dress like the one Geri Halliwell wore to the Brit Awards in 1997. But her absolute favourite childhood memory was going to watch the group at Manchester Arena when she was nine. Seeing the popstars performing on the massive stage, in their incredible costumes and in a gigantic venue with 15,000 people, had well and truly blown her mind and she had known then that music would be her life.

Of course, her original dream had been to be up there on the stage herself one day, singing her heart out into a microphone to a sea of adoring fans. The plan had been to form a girl group and then, after years of success, to achieve even greater things as a solo artist. Geri had done it. Beyoncé had done it.

And Olivia Harringay was going to do it.

But, as with most childhood dreams, the problem with achieving this became apparent as she got a little older and realised it wasn't enough to have a desire to be something. She needed other things. Scary, intangible things like talent, luck and opportunity. As she entered her teenage years, she realised that all those things were out of her hands. All she could do was work hard and hope.

Which is exactly what she did.

The group she had formed with her two best friends, Susie and Nicola, at the age of thirteen, imaginatively titled Girlz NoBoyz, was her first attempt at cracking the music industry. Using her father's basic recording equipment connected to the basic home PC, they had recorded themselves singing covers of current hits. The quality wasn't great, technically or vocally, but not wanting to dissuade his daughter, Olivia's father had helped her edit the clips together and copied them onto cassette tapes. She had posted the tapes to the addresses of as many record labels as she could find in the UK Business Directory book that she had begged her poor dad to buy her and had checked the mailbox every day for any returning correspondence.

But none had arrived.

Not to be deterred, she decided that the other girls in the group were probably holding her back and so she had vowed to begin her solo career earlier than planned at the age of fourteen. Calling herself 'Oliviayy', she dyed her auburn hair blonde, much to her mother's horror, and began recording the songs she had written while sitting in class at school. By then, technology was advancing at a rapid rate, and instead of posting out her music in the mail, she was able to use the website

Myspace to upload her songs for all the world to discover.

But nobody discovered them.

By the age of sixteen and having got nowhere with her music, Olivia had felt like giving up. But she couldn't leave music behind. She loved it too much. So instead of singing, she did the next best thing. She started talking.

Using the new and innovative online social media channels that were springing up on a seemingly daily basis, she began recording videos of herself reviewing the latest music in the charts. While this idea itself wasn't entirely original, the fact that she was doing it at such a young age was. Most people in the music scene using sites like YouTube in 2007 were either doing it to promote their own singing or were older, established journalists figuring out how to use online media to promote the companies they worked for. But Olivia was different. She wasn't some teenage girl singing in her bedroom. Nor was she a journalist in her twenties sitting in an office and awkwardly talking into the camera while wondering if the whole thing was just a waste of time. She was a sixteen, with a wicked sense of humour and a unique take on the current music scene.

Her videos began to get views, and within two years, she had been one of the most popular YouTubers in England. Certainly, she was one of the most popular YouTubers in Stockport, although the competition there hadn't been particularly strong unless you counted the old guy who was known for posting videos of himself shouting at passers-by from his bedroom window.

And nobody was counting him.

Olivia sat back in her chair and waited for the AMII Music logo to appear on her monitor so that she could log in and begin working through the mass of emails that had been building in her inbox all weekend. As she waited, she thought back to her first day at AMII, just over five years ago when she had been hired as a Digital Content Creator off the back of her popular YouTube platform. Some of her friends had advised her to turn down the job and continue making videos on her own, but while she had been earning good money from ad revenue on her content, she had never even considered the possibility of rejecting AMII. Because working there would give her access to the one thing that had been missing from her videos so far.

Actual music stars.

AMII gave her everything. Backstage passes. One-on-one interviews. Hilarious viral videos. She had done it all over the last five years, with some of the biggest music stars in the UK. Adele. Ed Sheeran. Stormzy. The list was endless. So too was the list of iconic music venues she had visited since being employed with the mega company. Abbey Road Studios, where The Beatles recorded their legendary tracks. The Roundhouse, famous for being the last venue at which Amy Winehouse performed. And Brixton Academy, where stars like Madonna played to intimate crowds before they went stratospheric. Not to mention the numerous tickets to massive gigs at Wembley Stadium, the O2 arena and of course annual attendance at the Brit Awards, the show she had watched in wonder all those years ago when the Spice Girls played their hits.

It had been an incredible five years, and she felt lucky to have experienced it all. But now she was hungry for more, and that meant getting this promotion. Because as a Senior Editor, she wouldn't just be attending some of the biggest music events with the biggest musicians in the UK. She would be hitting the world stage.

Europe. America. Asia.

Jay-Z. Kanye.

Beyoncé.

Not only that, but the basic backstage coverage and cliched Q & A interviews would be a thing of the past. In a senior role, she would be going much deeper into the music world, touring with and reporting on the real lives of the biggest music icons.

She was already aware that the first task for the newly-crowned Senior Editor at AMII Music would be to accompany German superstar DJ Nico Fire as he embarked on a whirlwind tour of seven countries in seven days in July. The electronic dance powerhouse was well known for his fist-pumping tracks, incredible live sets and partying lifestyle, so whoever got to record the details of such a tour would be getting privileged and much sought-after access. She could only cross her fingers and hope that it would be her.

As much as she loved London, she felt that it would do her good to get out of the country for a good proportion of the year and spend more time on the road. Not many people would prescribe going on drug-fuelled tours with drug-fuelled musicians to relax and clear your mind, but Olivia felt it would be just what she needed. The last couple of years had been rough for her, and as much as she loved her job and loved being in the capital, everything staying the same would only serve to remind her of what she had lost recently.

Both her parents, in just eighteen months. First her mum, who had succumbed to cancer after a short battle with the devastating disease. Then, as she was recovering from the shock of that first blow, her father had been struck down by a heart attack. While he survived the initial attack, his health never fully recovered and a stroke just over a year after that was the end. As an only child, Olivia had been extremely close to both of her parents. It had been because of their love, support and encouragement that she had found the confidence to persevere and eventually carve out a career for herself in the music industry when so many other people said it was impossible. They had been her two biggest supporters and would have bought whatever music she had put out if she had somehow made it as a musician, no matter how awful it most likely would have been. They had taken her to her first gigs and ignited her passion for music, and she had returned the favour by getting them backstage passes to meet some of their very own musical heroes when she had landed the job at AMII. The only thing that she regretted was not telling them both that as much as she idolised the popstars who she had seen singing on all those stages as a youngster, it had been they who had always been her true heroes.

Olivia sat up straight in her chair and took a deep breath, not allowing herself to think about her parents any more in case the tears started flowing. She would save that for later when she was back at home in the Greenwich flat that she had purchased outright with her inheritance money. If she got the promotion, she would probably rent it out while she was busy travelling around the world. It would be quite an earner for her. But she would give up the flat, and even the chance of the promotion, just to have one more day with her mum and dad.

She typed her password into her computer, mentally switching gear so that she felt ready for another busy day of work. She twirled a strand of her auburn hair as her emails loaded up, looking at the curls between her fingers and smiling again at the memory of the naïve young girl who had once dyed it blonde because she thought it gave her more chance of becoming a pop star.

She worked through her emails, scanning the long list for anything that seemed urgent. Thankfully there didn't seem to be anything that required immediate action, and she was just beginning to think it might be a gentle start to what would hopefully be her last week in this role when she saw one email that made her sit up even straighter in her chair.

Subject: *The next big thing? Andrew Ayata seems to think so...*

Olivia opened the email from her colleague Wendy and quickly read the contents:

Video of a busker in the Underground this morning. Seems to be getting some heat on social media and when I looked into it, I saw Andrew had not only liked the video but had added the guy in it. He's called

Will Robertson, and he's amazing. Could be worth checking out before someone else jumps on him?

Olivia felt the rush of adrenaline that often came with being on the verge of a potential scoop, as she clicked on the link in the email and started to watch the video of the busker in the Underground.

As the song played, her colleagues nearby stopped what they were working on and came around to see what she was watching. This guy was good. And Olivia knew the significance of Andrew Ayata's presence in the *Likes* column. He was one of the biggest music producers in the UK. He had judged on reality television shows and had helped to break some of the biggest acts on the planet. If he was keen on Will Robertson, then this could very well be the next big act to hit the music scene.

This could also be the final thing she needed to get her promotion over the line.

As she grabbed her work mobile and scrolled down her contacts list for the number to Andrew's studio, she felt pride at how far she had come in her young life. And despite everything bad that had happened to her recently, she knew deep down that somehow things were going to get better for her over the coming days.

The fact that the Russian stranger who got on her train every morning at Greenwich was planning to kill her in that same timespan was not something she could have comprehended as she looked ahead to many more years of life in her crazy little world of music.

Chantelle

08:40

Leicester Square Station, Central London

Chantelle Hughes couldn't believe how much money was in the guitar case by her feet. There were five-pound notes and even a couple of ten-pound notes, all sitting on a bed of gold and silver coins. If she had to guess, she would estimate there was at least fifty pounds' worth of cash in there, but it was going up by the second as more and more passers-by dropped their loose change into it.

Not that she was the reason for the money. That was solely down to the young man standing next to her, playing his guitar and working his way through a breath-taking medley of old and new pop songs. He was the reason for all the money being dropped at their feet and not for the first time today, she wished her friend was able to see exactly how well he was doing.

Unfortunately, that was out of the question. The busker was Will Robertson, with whom she had been friends since she and her family had moved in next door to his family eleven years ago. He was the same age as her, seventeen, and they had grown close over the years, sharing many things in common, like the same school, the same friendship group and the same strong desire to follow their dreams in life. Will wanted to be a musician. She wanted to be a social media star. The odds were against both of them.

But that wasn't going to stop them trying.

Will was certainly trying today, and she noticed the beads of sweat on his forehead as he closed his eyes and belted out the chorus to the Stereophonics hit 'A Thousand Trees'. And she would get back to trying to achieve her goal, as soon as she was out of the Underground and able to get a signal on her mobile phone. But for now, she didn't mind a few hours offline because being here with Will was absolutely worth the sacrifice.

She checked her watch and realised they had been down in the Underground for almost an hour. The time had flown by, mainly due to how entertainingly Will had been playing his instrument to the thousands of tourists and commuters who had walked past them before or after making their tube journeys. She was thrilled at how well he was doing, especially considering it was his first 'public' performance in almost six months. She knew how worried he had been about being in a busy place without being able to see what was happening around him, but she had assured him that she would be by his side the whole time and she had been true to her word. She hadn't been more than a couple of feet away from him since they had left his mum's home that morning and made the journey into Central London. And she wouldn't leave his side until they were back on their street later that day after his performance was over and they had treated themselves to a nice lunch somewhere in Leicester Square.

The majority of people watching Will busking as they made their way through the underground tunnel would have no idea why she was standing beside the guitarist. It didn't seem like she was bringing anything of value herself, simply standing next to the person who was doing all the work. But some people would notice if they looked more closely. They would see that Will's gaze wasn't catching theirs when they smiled at him. They would see that his eyes weren't being attracted by the high volume of foot traffic sweeping past him. And if they really paid attention, they would figure out that it was because Will was blind.

Then they would understand why she was there. She was supporting him. Her presence was providing comfort. But it went deeper than that. She knew that without her, he would still be in his bedroom, refusing to come out and share his incredible talent with the world. It had been she who had been able to persuade him to carry on with life after his family and friends had been unable to get through to him. He had been in a dark place, in all senses of the word, but thankfully, if a little surprisingly, she had been able to help him turn a corner and begin the process of returning to as much normality as possible.

But it hadn't been easy. It had been six months since Will had been struck down by a devastating condition that Chantelle still didn't properly understand. She could barely even say the name of it. Giant Cell Arteritis. Or something like that. Whatever it was called, it was a horrible thing to happen to anybody, never mind to one of her oldest and best friends; a young man who Chantelle considered to be one of the nicest people she had ever met.

When it had initially happened, she had been shocked to learn that Will was in hospital, and rushed to see him as quickly as she could. His mum was already there, and the poor woman looked terrified, trying to make sense of how something so horrendous could have happened to her son. He had gone suddenly blind while making a journey on the tube and his eyesight had failed to return since. The doctors said it was unlikely it ever would.

The news had been a huge shock to everybody, but they had all rallied around Will, determined to help him through one of the most difficult times anybody could ever experience. But understandably it had been brutal, and he had withdrawn into himself, shutting out the people who cared about him and essentially giving up on life.

Before the condition struck, he had been a happy, confident seventeen-year-old who had begun the first steps of sharing his true passion with the world. With the encouragement of Chantelle and others, he had begun busking on the streets of London and had been making good money doing so. With her social media savvy, she had created an Instagram account for him as a way to share his music with more people and possibly even attract the interest of record labels. It had all been going so well. The money from the busking was growing, the follower count on *@WillRobertsonMusic* was growing, and her feelings for her old friend were growing too.

Until tragedy had struck and brought it all to a crashing halt.

Six months was a long time, but today, finally, Will was back doing what he loved and proving to himself that he could continue his music career even without the benefit of sight. She felt so proud of him because she knew what he had been through to get here. Today had confirmed to her that he was as strong as she had told him he was in his bedroom all those times when he refused to come out and brave the world.

It had also confirmed one other thing.

She was in love with him.

She had noticed her feelings for Will developing into something stronger over the past year, as school ended and the powerful drive into adulthood commenced. Of course, she had always been fond of him. She had known him for most of her life. They had spent most of their childhood walking to school and back together. She was a couple of months older than he was, but even so, she had always thought of him as being like a big brother. He was taller than her, and she had always felt relaxed and protected when he was around.

But when they had left school at sixteen and moved on into sixth form college, she had started to see him differently. Instead of the dweeby school uniform she had been accustomed to seeing him in, he was now wearing his own clothes on their walks. His body had also filled out, and the early teenage spots he had sported across his face had begun to fade away. He was becoming more handsome with every passing month, and she now saw him very differently than she had before.

His blindness had only made her love him more. He was still the same on the outside, but internally he was more vulnerable now. She had seen him cry. She had heard his worst fears and darkest thoughts. She had held him when he had broken down in his bedroom on several occasions. He was a different person now, but, in some ways, he was a better person. She had seen all sides of him, the good and the bad, and through all that, her feelings had continued to intensify.

But of course, she hadn't told him about any of this. She didn't know how he felt, and she daren't risk damaging their lifelong friendship for what he might perceive as just a passing adolescent crush. Even if she knew it was much deeper than that. He had enough going on in his world right now without her complicating it with thoughts of romance. It must have taken all his mental strength to just to perform here today, and it was great to see he was pursuing his music again. That was the most important thing, and she didn't want to do anything that might send him off track again. She would be a loyal friend, support him when needed and run his social media account. Anything else would be pushed to the back of her mind.

But it was difficult. Especially when she had stood and watched him perform one of his own songs this morning, a song that she thought was one of the most beautifully written melodies she had ever heard.

It was called 'Demon in the Dark', and even though he hadn't explicitly said so, she knew it had been composed by Will as a way for him to process what it was like to go blind at such a young age. He had been shy about singing it today, but she had persuaded him, and she was glad she had. That song more than any other today had gained attention from the appreciative passers-by in the Underground. Several people had actually stopped while he was singing it and simply watched. Some had filmed his performance on their phones and most of the money in the guitar case had been contributed in response to that one song. Because it was so beautiful and heartfelt, and it had made her love him even more.

She watched him as he finished his latest song and saw him turn towards her.

"Can I have some more water?" he asked her, holding out his hand for the bottle she had been supplying him with for the last hour.

"Of course," she replied, quickly reaching down for the half-full bottle on the floor by her feet.

She handed it to him and watched him gulp down the liquid, soothing his overworked throat. She noticed him pull a face as he finished it and guessed what it was about.

"Warm?"

"Yeah, gross."

She laughed. *"Sorry, not much I can do about that. Unless you want me to bring an ice-box next time."*

He laughed and handed her back the empty bottle.

"If you're bringing an ice-box then there'd better be a couple of beers in there," he said giving her a wink.

Even though his gaze wasn't on her, it still gave her butterflies.

She smiled, glad to see he was chirpy and relaxed. He was clearly happy with his performance today, and most of all, contented enough with his situation, which was as good as could be expected.

She couldn't imagine how she would cope without such an important thing as sight, and she was finding his recent strength and positivity inspirational.

"What time is it?" he asked her as he strummed his pick across the strings of his guitar.

She checked her mobile.

"Eight forty."

"Wow that's gone quickly," he said, giving off a natural wave of energy that showed how delighted he was to be back doing his favourite thing in the world.

The time hadn't passed quite as quickly for her, just standing by while he performed, but she wasn't going to say anything that might dampen his mood. She would stay down here as long as he wanted to.

"Any chance you could get some more water?" he asked, fiddling with his strings and preparing for his next song.

"Yeah of course, I'll just close the case," she said, crouching down to gather up the guitar case full of money.

"No, leave it," he told her. *"I'll keep playing while you go."*

She paused and looked up at him. His eyes were unfocused and gazing into the distance, but his face was happy and relaxed.

"Are you sure you'll be okay on your own?" she asked, concerned.

"I've got to try it sometime. I can't have you standing beside me for the rest of my career, can I?" he said, laughing.

"You can if you end up at the Brits," she replied. She would give anything to go to the huge music awards show for British talent and to be there with Will really would be the icing on the cake.

He laughed again and nodded.

"If I get to the Brits, I promise I'll take you with me," he assured her.

"I'll hold you to that," she said, preparing to leave him but still unsure.

"I'll go to the shop in the station, so I'll be back in less than five minutes," she promised him, which to her seemed a long time to leave him alone on his first day busking blind in a busy train station.

"Cool, I might play Demon in the Dark again when you get back," he said, smiling in her general direction.

"I hope so," she said, before giving him a reassuring touch on the arm and heading for the escalators.

She looked back at her brilliant friend as she ascended the escalator to the ticket hall and though she still felt worried about leaving him, she knew he would be fine. He would keep singing and entertaining the public and, as most people wouldn't realise that he was blind, it was unlikely that anybody would try and steal the money.

She reached the ticket hall and headed for the small newsagents that was built into the station to service the many travellers passing through the station with drinks, snacks and newspapers. Once there, she took two bottles of water out of the fridge and grabbed a couple of chocolate bars for good measure.

They could use the sugar rush.

As she stood in line and waited to pay, she glanced at the various newspapers displayed on the shelves. The headlines were about the usual things. Politics. The Royal Family. A celebrity scandal. One of the tabloids had a photo of an exhausted fireman below the headline **FIRE SERVICES UP IN FLAMES,** and she leaned forward a little closer to read what it was about. Her uncle had been a fireman before retiring last year, and she knew he had always been complaining about how they were treated by the government. She read on and saw the article was about further cutbacks to the fire services with the potential loss of up to 5,000 jobs across the UK.

She sighed as she reached the till and dropped her snacks onto the counter. She was young, and she didn't know much about how to run a country, but she knew one thing; cutting jobs in the emergency services surely wasn't the right way to go. There would come a time when everybody needed their help.

It was only a matter of time.

Curtis

08:41

Turner Crescent, Brockmore Estate,

North London

Curtis Bridge didn't know how the fire had started, but he hoped that nobody was in the burning buildings he was trying to control right now.

He maintained his position to the left of the main blaze and continued to direct the stream of water pumping from his hose at the upstairs window of the flaming flat. Judging by what he had seen when he and his crew had arrived on the scene at 08:38, the fire had begun in an upper storey of one of the many flats that lined this street but had quickly spread into the adjoining properties on each side. While it had been clear that the address identified as the source of the fire was impossible to access, that hadn't stopped his colleagues from performing their duties and trying. But the strength of the blaze had forced them all back and, by now, it would have been impossible to save anybody inside anyway. But the adjacent properties, while alight, had not yet been devoured by the inferno and Curtis was one of the firemen who had been tasked with holding the spread of raging flames at bay while the others went inside to check for anybody trapped inside their homes.

He glanced down the street at where his hose was connected to the water hydrant and then at the large crowd of concerned members of the public who had gathered beyond the perimeter that the fire crews had established upon arrival. All other residents of the properties on the same side of the street as the fire had been evacuated, but worryingly, one resident had told them that he knew of an elderly woman who lived in the flat beside the main blaze and he hadn't seen her leave yet. His colleagues were currently working to locate her, but he remained focused on his job, which was to control the fire and prevent it from getting any worse until the back-up crews arrived.

This was fast becoming a major blaze across multiple residences and would not be quick to put out. But it was precisely what he was trained to do and what he had signed up for when he had first applied to become a firefighter nineteen years earlier. Back then, he had been a fresh-faced and naïve twenty-five-year-old, seeking direction and purpose in life and becoming a fireman had helped him find those things. But now, in his forties, battle-scarred from some of his experiences in the job and facing the financial pressure of looming job cuts ahead, he had begun to think he had made a mistake becoming a firefighter.

It was a key job in society, forming part of the main triumvirate of emergency services, along with the police and the ambulance teams but you wouldn't think it from the way the government treated them. Cutbacks, lack of resources, job losses, closures, he had seen it all during his time in the job. He'd also learnt that the majority of people on the frontline like him weren't paid well for their work and it was only the top chiefs who made big money. Those who risked their lives for the public were appreciated by those they helped but seemingly not by those in power. Never mind a good wage and job security; they were lucky to get a pat on the back and a thank you. He had already been part of two fire stations that had been shut down during his employment with the London Fire Brigade, and while he had been lucky to be moved on to other stations, he didn't need to read today's newspapers to know that more cuts were forecast for the fire crews in future.

The blaze raged on as he and his teammates worked to control it and the sound of sirens in the distance told them all that help was on the way. But these back-up crews wouldn't be able to help him if he lost his job. They had enough worries of their own to deal with. That's why he had been thinking that it was time to get out of this line of work.

Before he was forced to.

Or before something even worse happened...

It had been no surprise to him to learn that he would be putting his life on the line every time he responded to a call-out, but he would be lying if he said he hadn't completely underestimated the toll that the job would take on his mental health. He'd noticed the change in his moods over the last few years and knew it wasn't just down to just getting older. It was the consequence of the things he had seen.

The fires from which he had saved people from.

But mainly the fires from which he hadn't been able to save people.

The night of Wednesday 11th October 2014 was one that Curtis would never forget. He was working the last day of his rotational shift before two weeks of paid leave. He and his wife Karen were really looking forward to travelling to Australia to visit their son, Michael, who was backpacking the country alone. The night had been quiet, and Curtis had been thinking that he was going to get his wish for an uneventful last shift before his holiday. But alas it was not to be.

The call to his station came at 1:05 am with reports of a fire at a flat in Camden. They had responded quickly and were on their way when they heard on the radio that the fire was spreading to surrounding flats within the building. That had been the first moment of concern for Curtis and his team as they sped through the quiet London streets towards the site of the blaze. Normally, fires like the one described in the original call-out stayed contained within the flat where they had started. In fact, it was a requirement that blocks of flats should be designed and constructed in such a way that in the event of a fire breaking out, the damage would be confined. It was the reason people were sometimes told to stay inside a burning building if they couldn't see smoke.

Because the fire shouldn't be able to spread to them.

But upon arrival, it had been clear that the fire was spreading, and fast. Thankfully, the block of flats was small, only five floors in total, but the fire had begun on the ground floor and was quickly taking hold across the base of the building. While on paper it would be easier to tackle a blaze closer to the ground than one at the top of the structure, the fact that it was spreading rapidly meant that if they weren't successful in quickly smothering it, the people above it would be trapped.

Curtis was one of the first responders, and his crew was tasked with going inside and tackling the fire directly. The second and third crews that were right behind them would work on controlling the blaze from the outside. Of course, this was what he was trained for, and while he hadn't been concerned when they were heading inside the building, it quickly became apparent that this wasn't a normal fire.

Upon arrival in the reception area of the building, and through the thick black smoke that was enveloping the room, he noticed the water sprinklers on the roof weren't activated. That would have bought them valuable time and helped weaken the blaze, but, as it was, the fire was spreading without restraint.

Within minutes, visibility was almost down to zero, and the decision was made over the radio for Curtis's team to focus on rescuing the residents who were still inside and leave the fire-fighting to those crew members outside.

Curtis and his brave colleagues had headed up the pitch-black staircase and were relieved to see some residents already on their way down. But due to the poor visibility, they were being escorted out for their safety, and Curtis soon saw his crew dwindle until it was just himself and two others. They reached the top floor and began banging on doors in an attempt to wake up the people sleeping on the other side of them. The fact that it was so quiet up there was another concern. Because it meant the fire alarm wasn't working. What could have been a simple fire was quickly becoming a recipe for disaster.

Curtis had reached the end of the top floor corridor and had been relieved to see some of the doors opening and the residents emerging in their pyjamas. He had shouted at them all to wrap a wet cloth or towel around their mouths and head for the stairs, and they had all done well to take his advice without argument. But Curtis had noticed that one door was still closed and it was while he was banging on it again that he was told the reason why it hadn't opened yet. Apparently, the resident inside was a ninety-year-old man called Albert, and he was completely deaf.

Without wasting a second Curtis had kicked down the door.

He had quickly been able to locate the elderly resident in his bedroom, and after almost giving the poor old chap a heart attack when he woke him up, he had tried to get him to follow. But Albert was frail, and walking was difficult for him. There was no time to waste. Curtis picked up the man and carried him towards the door.

Heading down the smoke-filled staircase with Albert in his arms, he had almost lost his balance and sense of direction several times. He had also known that with every step they descended, they were getting closer to the fire from which they were trying to escape.

The old man's coughing prompted Curtis to move with increased urgency, and they had reached the second floor in quick time. At that point, Curtis had been confident that they were going to make it out in time, but as he headed down to the first floor, he tripped on a discarded piece of clothing on the staircase and fell to the ground.

He and Albert had both felt the full impact of their bodies hitting the concrete floor, and as he lay there trying to get his breath back, unable to see anything around him, Curtis had experienced a panic attack.

It had been unlike anything he had been through before and even with all his training he had found it impossible to get his breathing back under control. In his panic he had even removed his helmet, exposing himself to the acrid black smoke that engulfed them. He hadn't admitted it to anybody since that day, but he had honestly believed he was going to die on that staircase.

Fortunately, his colleagues had gone back into the building after he had failed to emerge and discovered him and Albert on the ground, struggling for air. They had both been rescued, and thankfully Albert had made a full recovery. Curtis had even attended his 91st birthday party five months later at the care home into which the old man had been moved following his ordeal.

But what happened that night in 2014 had stayed with Curtis forever. He had witnessed worse things during his time as a firefighter. He had seen death. He had seen devastation. There had been plenty of occasions when he had only just made it out of burning buildings in time. But that night was the worst because he knew that if he had died, it wouldn't have been because of the fire, or bad luck, or a refusal to leave someone behind.

It would have been because his mind had betrayed him.

That panic attack had left him living in constant fear of the next one. And there had been several, though fortunately none in the line of duty. They would come to him during the night when he would wake up scrambling for breath and his wife would grab his arm in fright. When it was over, he would tell her he was okay and that it was just a bad dream. But he knew the truth. He was struggling mentally and most of all he was afraid that the next panic attack would happen when he was in the midst of fire-fighting, at a time when it really was a matter of life or death.

Curtis watched as the support crews began working on the blaze beside him and he saw that their efforts were quickly having an impact on the strength of the fire. The flat it had started in was going to be a burnt-out shell, there was no doubt about that, but at least they were getting a hold of it now. But he still hadn't seen his colleagues emerge from the flat next door and began to worry that something was wrong inside.

Suddenly he saw two firefighters coming out of the flat but what he saw next almost caused him to drop the hose he was holding.

They were carrying an elderly woman between them, moving her to safety. She was unconscious, and her clothes were stained black from the smoke. He could only hope they had got to her in time.

As the paramedics at the scene began their checks on the rescued woman, Curtis overheard two police officers talking only yards away from him.

He heard them say something about a neighbour reporting a man leaving the scene of the fire only moments before the explosion. Arson suspect. Possible murder suspect if any bodies were discovered inside. Then he heard them describe the man.

Tall and thin.

Blue baseball cap.

Bag over his shoulder.

Heading north in the direction of the train station.

Becky

08:42

St Pancras International,
North London

Becky Davis scanned the tickets and allowed the pleasant woman and her young child to pass her and head for the 08:45 Eurostar service to Paris. The queue to board was a big one, as it usually was on a Monday morning, consisting mostly of business travellers heading to France for meetings and pitches. But there were a few tourists dotted about in the queue. They were easy to spot. They were the only ones not wearing suits, and usually, they were the only ones smiling.

Thankfully, there were no issues with her or her colleague Richard's ticket scanner this morning, so they were getting the travellers through the barriers quickly, in time to board the train that was leaving in a few minutes' time. Some days their electronic scanners would fail, and they would have to inspect each ticket manually, which always took more time and made a dull job even more tedious. But today things were moving as quickly as they should be and all in all, Becky thought, this wasn't the worst start to a week that she'd ever had. She hadn't even got drunk this weekend, so there were no remnants of a hangover affecting her body and all told, she felt great, which was a lot more than could be said for poor Richard.

"How we doing there, partner?" she asked him, during a momentary gap in the queue.

"Bloody awful," he replied, sweat noticeably blooming on his forehead.

Just because Becky hadn't consumed alcohol this weekend didn't mean that Richard had shown as much restraint and he was clearly suffering the consequences.

"I told you before, you're too old to be carrying on as you do," she teased him, something she liked to do at every opportunity. He was sensitive about his age, having just passed forty and with thinning hair and ever-deepening wrinkles on his forehead, but she didn't have much sympathy. She was closer to fifty herself, and while she felt fine, she would often pretend to Richard that it was all downhill from forty.

"I'm not too old, I just didn't sleep well," he offered as a feeble line of defence.

"Sleep's the first thing to go as you get older" she continued, smirking at how easy it was to wind him up. *"When you get to my age, you're lucky if you get five hours a night."*

"You're joking?" he asked, slightly terrified.

"I wish I were. Some nights I'm wide awake until two am, other nights I wake up before dawn and that's me done. It's quite common, I think."

Now Richard looked really worried, and Becky thought she might have gone a little too far in pulling his leg. But then he got his familiar smile back and shook his head.

"Sorry Granny, but I'm not buying it. You can't fool me," he told her before scanning another passenger's ticket.

Becky smiled as she too served another customer. She loved working with Richard. It had been two years now since he had joined the company and her shifts had flown by whenever she had been paired with the younger man. He was something she had needed in her life but hadn't realised she was missing until she found it.

A gay best friend.

Richard was funny, energetic, and positive. He was well-groomed and smart. He even had better hair than she did. She would probably have had a crush on him if he weren't into men and she wasn't married to one herself. She loved working with him, and she loved drinking with him at the many bars around the station whenever they had the time in their busy diaries to grab a bottle of wine or two after their shifts ended.

Because Richard was unlike all her other friends. They were all her age, pushing fifty and all female. Their lives were all similar. Married. Working boring jobs. One eye on retirement, the other on potential grandkids. Conversations about the latest happenings on EastEnders or Coronation Street. Or what work they were thinking of having done on the house. Not that it bothered her. She loved her female friends and had known most of them since she was at high school back in the eightie's. It was just that their lives were exactly the same as hers, and so she felt like every get-together was predictable. Nice, but predictable. But then she had met Richard, and it had been like being given the keys to a whole new world.

For a man who was hitting middle age, he behaved like someone who had just left university. He had an enthusiasm and vigour for life that she hadn't felt or witnessed in her own social circle for decades. While her weekends consisted of housework, Sunday lunches with the family and maybe a wine and cheese night with another couple, his weekends sounded more like episodes from a television comedy-drama. Multiple flings. Chance encounters. Risqué rendezvous. Secret clubs. Affairs. Drama. Gossip. And many hilarious stories that had made her cry tears of laughter and almost spill her wine when she had heard them.

As a brunette, she had always wondered if it was true when she heard people say that blondes had more fun. But now she knew the real truth.

Gay people had more fun.

After all that she had learnt from listening to Richard over the past couple of years, there was simply no denying it. Any drama in her life or in the lives of her heterosexual friends just paled in comparison to the kind of action Richard's life consisted of on a seemingly daily basis.

She'd never forgotten the time he told her about his date with a man he had met online called Fernando. Richard had been expecting a tanned, Portuguese man with a passion for exotic dancing and even more exotic cocktails. After all, that had been what the stranger's dating profile had suggested. But when he had gone to the arranged venue to meet his date, Richard had discovered that Fernando was not a tanned Portuguese man who enjoyed exotic dancing and cocktails. He was a fifty-seven-year-old truck driver from Yorkshire who had suffered a mid-life crisis, dumped his wife and decided to try his chances in the gay community. He had made up an online persona to improve his odds of getting a date and Becky had fought back tears of laughter as Richard had gone on to tell her about his date with Fernando, who, it turned out, was actually called Fred.

They had met in a pub called *The Cock*, which despite being named after a hen and having nothing to do with any particular sexual orientation, had been affectionately adopted by those in the gay community as a good place for first dates.

After getting over his surprise that the supposedly thirty-eight-year-old Fernando was actually a bloke in his fifties called Fred, Richard had decided that it was still worth pursuing, so had agreed to stay and have a drink.

He had ordered his favourite cocktail, 'The Lucky Cock', which was a fruity mix of vodka, rum and apple juice and also proved that despite not intending on running a pub that would be used as a gay venue, the landlord had certainly figured out a way to cash in on his circumstances. Richard had asked Fred to choose his own cocktail from the menu, and there had been plenty of choice. Drinks with names like 'The Fruity Cock', 'The Forbidden Cock', or the most popular and most expensive one on the menu, 'Lock, Cock and Two Smoking Barrels'. But in the end Fred had just opted for a pint of bitter.

Becky had then listened in hysterics as Richard had gone on to tell her about the rest of his date with Fred and how it had become clear that the older man was certainly going through some confusing times. Fred, or Fernando (it was hard to keep up), had told Richard that he had been married for over thirty years but when his wife had suddenly left him for another man he had suffered a crisis of confidence and questioned everything he had ever known about his sexuality. Richard had assured him that if he were truly gay, he would have known about it by now, but Fred said he wasn't so sure and, ever the experimentalist, Richard had offered to help him find out by taking him on a whirlwind tour of some of the biggest and best gay venues in London that night.

Becky, whose own Saturday night that weekend had consisted of staying in with a cup of tea and working her way through several episodes of Emmerdale that she had recorded onto her Sky box, had listened on in amazement in the next part of the story.

Richard and his new friend Fred had left *The Cock* and hailed a taxi. Their first port of call was a trendy wine bar called *Paulo's Vineyard* in Soho, and while Richard stressed how great this place was for meeting men in an intimate atmosphere, Fred had been disappointed to see that there weren't any pints of bitter on the menu.

Their second stop had been at a nightclub called *Come Underground*, which was built into the body of a disused Underground station and was basically one massive rave in a tiny room just below street level.

Richard persuaded Fred to do shots of Patron, and while the older man was seemingly enjoying himself a little more than at the previous venue, they had decided to move on when Fred had become alarmed at some of the activity going on in the gents' toilets.

It was 2 am by the time they reached the club in Shoreditch that Richard had chosen as the final venue in their whistle-stop tour. Simply titled *Throb*, he had told Fred that this was the last resort on a night out; a place to go when finding a man felt imperative, but all other options had been exhausted. Apparently, it had been easy to see why. The dancefloor was just a glistening mass of topless, sweaty men, and the music was just one long, pounding baseline that shook the walls and made conversation impossible.

Richard had shown Becky a photo taken inside the club that night of Fred, standing on the dancefloor in his buttoned-up shirt, pint of bitter in hand and a confused look on his face, while surrounded by topless men who were half his age. She had laughed so much she had snorted wine through her nose.

The two men had stayed there until 4 am, when Fred had decided that this lifestyle actually wasn't for him after all and asked to leave. Ever the good host, Richard had taken Fred for a greasy kebab before putting him in a taxi and sending him home, but not before testing the man by giving him a quick peck on the lips. Fred had immediately blushed and thanked Richard, before falling into the car and passing out with his face pressed against the passenger side window.

All in all, it had been a pretty standard Saturday night in the world of Richard Bateman, but to Becky, it had been one of the greatest stories she had ever heard. And every time she met him, there was another story, just as crazy and unpredictable as the last. Today would be no different, and she would no doubt hear all about what he had gotten up to at the weekend when his hangover was a little more under control, and they had ensured all the passengers rushing towards them had made it onto the train that was about to leave their platform.

She checked her watch and saw that the train was due to leave in one minute's time. Thankfully, all the passengers seemed to have boarded now, and she and Richard were just about to close the barriers and head back up the gangway when they saw a tall man sprinting towards them.

He was wearing a blue baseball cap and had a backpack over his shoulder. Probably a tourist heading to Paris for an impromptu bit of sightseeing. But his train would be leaving any second, and he would do well to make it now.

"Somebody's cutting it fine," Richard said as he and Becky watched the man racing desperately towards them.

Becky checked her watch again. The train was due to depart any moment. She pre-emptively opened the barriers and got her ticket scanner ready again in order to give this man the best chance possible of making his train. The odds weren't in his favour, but she had to try.

The man finally made it to them but didn't stop, passing straight through the barriers without showing his ticket.

"Hey!" Richard shouted, and the man suddenly stopped, the backpack almost falling from his shoulder as he did.

"You got a ticket mate?" Richard asked him, eyeing the man suspiciously.

"Yes, I have ticket," the man replied, in a thick Eastern European accent.

"Well, do you feel like showing it to us?" Richard asked, doing his best impression of a ticket inspector who was trying not to get too irritated by a stupid passenger.

The man was breathing heavily as he held out his ticket towards Becky, who in turn held out her electronic scanner over the barcode.

The machine bleeped and confirmed that everything was ok.

"Thank you," Richard said sarcastically as they watched the man sprinting towards the train.

He only just made it on board. The doors closed seconds behind him, the whistle was blown, and the train slowly came to life, moving away from the platform and beginning its journey towards France via the Channel Tunnel.

"I never understand why people leave it to the last minute," Becky said as they watched the train disappearing out of the station.

"That's because you're never late for anything," Richard said. *"Why would you be when you're in bed every night by nine?"*

"Oi, cheeky," she said, hitting him playfully across the arm as they turned and walked back along the platform.

They continued chatting all the way back to the main station, where they would grab a cup of coffee and a quick five-minute break in the staff room before returning to their day's work. When they did return, they would have to speak with two police officers who were making enquiries at the station about a man seen leaving the scene of an earlier explosion in the area, which had claimed at least one life so far. They would assume they would be unable to help with the enquiries until they were shown a photograph of the man in question when they would realise that it was the same man they had helped board the train to Paris at the last second.

If only they had known not to let him through.

Now he had left the country and was most likely gone forever.

Ali

08:43

Eurostar: London - Paris

Ali Mehmet plugged his laptop charger into the socket connected to his table and hit the power button. As his device sprang into life, he looked around the First Class carriage at his fellow passengers.

They were much like him. Business professionals heading to Paris to begin a work trip, or maybe making their way home after completing their work in London. Also like him, they wore business attire, though he noted that none of them were as smartly dressed as he was. Nor were their laptops or company mobiles as expensive and as modern as his. As he logged into his computer, he wondered what some of these other people did for work.

Were their tasks as important as his? Did they make as much money as he did? Were their services as much in demand as his were?

It was doubtful, and he felt smug about that as his fingers trickled across his keyboard and logged in to his company's secure network. It was the secure network run by the recruitment company he had started when he was just twenty-five. The same company that nine years later had just been nominated as one of the most Influential Recruitment Agencies in the UK. Ali would find out if they would be given the award when he attended the ceremony at the Dorchester Hotel next week, but it wasn't as if his company didn't have enough awards to its name already.

Recruitment Agency of the Year 2016 and *2017. Recruiter Leader of the Year 2018. Most Innovative Recruitment Agency 2018.* And Ali's personal favourite. *Recruitment Industry Entrepreneur of the Year 2019.* It was his favourite because he hadn't had to share that one with his employees.

That one was all his.

The shelves in his office at Champion Recruiters were full of golden statuettes signifying how far he had brought the company he had founded less than a decade earlier. But that didn't mean he didn't want more awards and he was positive that next Wednesday he would be standing on a stage in his tuxedo accepting another big trophy on behalf of himself and his 2,000 employees.

But those thoughts were for another day as he needed to focus on the task at hand. He was on his way to Paris on an impromptu but important trip. His job was to convince a Frenchman called Steven Dacort that his next job should be as the Head of Treasury at the Iranian National Bank in London, a job that came with a huge pay packet and a similarly eye-watering bonus for the person who found somebody to fill the role. Ali had his sights set firmly on that bonus and so determined was he to beat the competition and secure it for himself that he had cancelled the rest of his day's meetings and was making a speculative trip across the English Channel to ensure he got it over the line.

He had identified Steven as an ideal candidate for the role three weeks ago and had been in regular contact with the Frenchman during that time in an attempt to persuade him to come to London for an interview. But Steven had rejected his advances, saying that although he was flattered to be deemed the number one candidate for the role, he wasn't sure if moving to another country was right for his wife and two young children at this time. Ali had suggested other candidates to the Iranians, but none of them had impressed, and when he heard that they were engaging the services of other recruitment companies to find a candidate, he knew he had to act fast.

The plan was to surprise Steven at his office in Paris, take the man out for a high-end lunch and give him his best sales pitch. If all went well then he would then head back to the UK later that day with a promise from the Parisian that he would at least attend an interview in London in the coming week. Ali felt confident that once Steven was in the offices of the Iranian National Bank, he would not be able to resist the job offer they would have put together for him. Even if he did, they would likely just increase their offer right then and there, such was their access to funds, at which point surely Steven would realise that the attractive package made the prospect of disrupting his family worthwhile.

And leaving Ali significantly better off.

Ali looked up from his laptop and saw an attractive blonde woman taking her seat across the aisle from him. She wore a dark blouse, pinstriped skirt and black heels with points that were just short enough to keep them suitable for business but just long enough to get the attention of every man she would encounter that day. Just like Ali, the second she was in her seat then her laptop was open, and her phone was placed beside it. She was clearly there to work too, and while he appreciated seeing the focused drive of a fellow professional, he wasn't going to let the opportunity to speak to her pass him by. He was a busy man, and he didn't have time for dating. But he had time to collect numbers and see if it led to anything fun.

As the train pulled away from the platform and made its way out of the station, Ali replied to an email from one of his employees, while keeping one eye on the woman, who was, by now, typing away on her keyboard. He wasn't going to speak too soon, that would make him seem a little desperate. And he needed her to notice him first before any interaction took place so that she was primed when he did speak. With that in mind, he picked up his phone and made a quick call to his PA.

"Hey Kirsty, yeah I'm on the way. Just a quick one, can you rearrange my 5 o'clock with Orion. Depending on how this afternoon goes, I may stay the night in Paris and use it as an opportunity to work on some more business."

He knew he had been speaking loudly enough to get the woman's attention and as he looked out of his window at the English capital rolling by, he caught sight of her in the reflection of the glass looking in his direction.

"That's great, thanks Kirsty. Send me the minutes of the team meeting when you have them, and

I'll let you know if I need a hotel for tonight as soon as I can."

He hung up and placed his phone back down on the table beside his laptop. As he did, he looked over and saw that the woman had returned her attention back to the screen in front of her.

"Sorry if I interrupted your work," he said to her as she typed.

"It's fine," she replied, without looking up.

He was just about to speak again when he saw the woman in the red and blue uniform pushing the trolley into the carriage a few seats ahead. There were many perks to travelling First Class, like having a table to yourself and more space to store your belongings, but the best one by far was the service. Those in the standard carriages would have to get out of their seats and visit the on-board shop if they wanted any refreshments, but here he could simply sit back and wait for it all to be brought to him.

Ali reclined in his seat and smiled as the woman with the trolley reached his table and paused beside him.

"Can I get you anything, Sir?" she asked him, ever so politely.

He noticed she was wearing a rather extreme amount of makeup, but he appreciated the effort she had made and decided that he would give her a good tip when it was time to pay.

"Please, ladies first," he replied, motioning towards the blonde woman who sat across from him.

The woman looked up from her laptop and smiled at the kind gesture.

"Thank you. I'll have a black coffee, please," she said, checking her phone and reading the notifications that had popped up on her screen in the short time she had been travelling.

Ali watched the woman in the uniform serve the coffee before she finally turned back to him and asked for his order again.

"Is it too early for wine?" he asked the woman with a cheeky grin on his face and a posture so relaxed that he knew she wouldn't refuse him.

"That's up to you, Sir," she replied, smiling back.

Ali made a big show of checking the time on his Rolex watch before pretending to ponder his decision a moment longer.

"What would you do?" he asked the woman serving him, noticing that the blonde businesswoman was now watching them.

"Me? Well, erm...I don't know" the woman said, blushing a little but enjoying her conversation with the attractive man in the First Class carriage.

"I think you'd have a little drink wouldn't you, Emma?" he said, referencing the name on the badge that was pinned to her red and blue blouse and which also bore the logo of the train company.

Emma laughed, just loud enough to make some of the other people in the carriage look up from their work. But Ali didn't care; he was enjoying the harmless conversation and, most of all, he was enjoying the fact that the blonde woman nearby was still watching them.

"I guess I would," she eventually conceded, and Ali smiled and nodded.

"Go on then Emma, you've twisted my arm. I'll have a red wine."

He winked at the woman as she opened her trolley and pulled a miniature bottle of red wine from one of the compartments.

"Do you have anything a little bigger?" he asked her before she'd had a chance to open it.

"Erm, well yes, but the bigger bottles aren't included with your ticket unfortunately," she told him.

"That's absolutely fine," he assured her as he pulled his wallet from his pocket and slid his black corporate card out. He knew his card was going to take a beating today while he wined and dined Steven, so it might as well get a little warm-up now.

He watched as the woman serving him took a larger bottle of wine out of the trolley and placed it on his table along with one small glass.

"Thank you," he said as he handed her the corporate card and she busied herself with the card reader machine nearby.

He unscrewed the cap on the wine and poured himself a healthy measure before entering his pin number and asking for the receipt. With the transaction complete, the women thanked him for his business. But before she could walk away, Ali had one final request.

"Sorry, could I get an extra glass please?" he asked.

"Oh, of course," the woman said and stopped, taking another small glass out of the trolley and placing it on his now quite crowded table.

"Thank you," he said and gave her another smile as she finally moved on down the carriage.

By now, the blonde woman had gone back to her work, but this didn't deter Ali. He poured a second glass of wine, then reached across and placed it on her table beside her laptop.

"I thought you might fancy something stronger than a coffee," he said as she stopped typing and looked at the wine.

"I'm okay thank you," she said, trying to be polite but failing to disguise her disapproval. It wasn't even 9 am yet and despite how appealing the wine looked in comparison to her coffee she was clearly a little too uptight to accept it.

"It's a two-hour journey, you might change your mind," he said, raising his eyebrows flirtatiously and taking a large gulp from his own glass.

"I doubt it," she said stiffly, returning to her work but not before Ali had detected signs of stress in the sharply-dressed woman.

Still, he decided to persevere with the conversation.

"What takes you to Paris?" he asked, eager to learn more about her if only to make the rest of the journey pass by more quickly than if he just spent it replying to emails.

"The train," she snapped back expertly, displaying a wry sense of humour that only served to increase his attraction towards her.

"Good one," Ali replied, raising his glass to her in respect.

She looked up from her laptop and finally smiled, showing a more pleasant side above the cold professional veneer she had been careful to offer so far.

"I'm going to visit someone," she told him, taking a sip from her coffee and glancing out of the window as the train passed through the outer reaches of London.

"Very mysterious," Ali replied, closing his laptop to show her that she had his full attention.

She took the bait and opened up a bit. *"I'm a head-hunter. I'm going to see if I can persuade someone to leave their current job and take up a new one with my client."*

Ali's eyes lit up as he heard this.

"Interesting. I'm doing exactly the same thing. Well, I'm not a head-hunter per se, but I own my own recruitment company. So, I kind of have to do a bit of everything, you know?"

He took out his wallet again and removed one of his business cards before reaching over and offering it to her.

"Thanks," she said, accepting it. *"Champion Recruiters. I've heard of you guys. You've won a few awards, haven't you?"*

"One or two," Ali said, smirking. *Do you have one?"* he asked her, aware that as soon as he got her card, he would have her number, which would make setting up a date with this attractive woman all the more straightforward.

"Yeah, sure," she replied and reached into her handbag.

She pulled a card out from her purse and handed it to him, and he turned it over to read the front. Its light-yellow surface was imprinted with attractive black type, which spelt out her name: Kirsten

Reeves. But before he saw anything else, he noticed the name of the company she represented. Reeves & Gallagher. He recognised that name too. They were major players in the finance industry and the company that many corporations used to help fill key roles in their organisations. He also knew that Reeves & Gallagher had been in contact with the Iranians about the Head of Treasury position.

"Who are you going to see in Paris?" he asked, suddenly aware that this chance encounter might not be as lucky as he had thought.

"Who are you going to see in Paris?" she replied, trying to read his face for the answer to the same question he had already asked her.

As the train raced out of London and across the green fields of Kent on its mission towards the English coast, both Ali and Kirsten drank their wine quickly and kept conversation to a minimum as they realised that they were both going to Paris to see the same man.

Lindsey

08:44

Waterloo, Central London

Lindsey Beattie stared at the enormous coffee machine on the kitchen counter and tried to figure out how to get it to work. She twisted one dial. A second. A third. Nothing happened. Then she finally figured out how to make the hot water work, but that wasn't much use without the coffee to go with it. When she twisted the fourth dial and got blasted with a vat of hot steam, she decided to give up and grabbed a bottle of water from the fridge instead.

If she was going to be working here full time, then she would have to figure it out at some point, but for now, she was too sleepy to waste another second on the machine. Plus, she was due in her induction meeting in the main conference room in one minute's time, so she had to get moving.

It wouldn't look good to be late on her first day.

She carried her water out of the kitchen and headed across the busy open-plan office to what she had been told was the conference room. As she went, she noticed that most of the employees here were already hard at work, logged in and making phone calls or sending emails. The majority were young, in their twenties or thirties, and there were even a few people who appeared younger than her own age of twenty-two. That boded well for the office socials that had been mentioned during one of her interviews. She had been told this was a vibrant, energetic place to work, and it certainly seemed that way from what she had seen so far.

Even if she wasn't feeling particularly vibrant or energetic at this time on a Monday morning.

She entered the conference room and saw two other people sitting at the rectangular table that dominated the interior. One was male, chubby and appeared to be in his mid-twenties. The other was female, short hair, possibly closer to thirty. All seemed okay, until she noticed what they were wearing.

Suits.

Which was a problem. Because she wasn't wearing one. She suddenly felt massively underdressed in her blouse and dark jeans, but she had been told in the interview that the dress code was casual. It was also looking like it was going to be another hot day in London, so the thought of wearing a suit hadn't even occurred to her. She already felt out of her comfort zone. Only a few weeks earlier, she had been living a world of beaches, bikinis and unemployment during her travelling days; now she had been thrust into the world of meetings, timekeeping and uncomfortable clothing. She looked around the room at the two power-dressers who were eyeing her up and down suspiciously.

"Hi," she offered, as a way to break the silence.

"Oh hi," the girl replied, then instantly went back to looking at her phone.

The guy simply waved his hand in her direction then went back to staring at the wall.

So much for vibrant and energetic.

Lindsey looked at the ten vacant chairs around the table, picked one and sat down, close enough to the other two people not to be rude, but leaving enough space between them not to be weird. The silence was back and not for the first time today Lindsey cursed the fact that her university and travelling days were over and that she would probably spend the rest of her life bouncing between awkward situations like this one.

"I'm Lindsey," she said, trying to get some form of conversation going with her new colleagues, if only to make the next few moments more bearable.

The guy snapped out of his trance and looked at her again.

"Dale," he replied.

"Nice to meet you," she said with a smile.

He nodded his head at her and looked back at the wall.

Dale seemed to be a lot of fun.

Lindsey glanced at her other new colleague, whose thumbs were still flying across her phone; it didn't seem like she had heard them at all.

"Cool," Lindsey muttered quietly.

A depressingly familiar silence returned to the room but, mercifully, was interrupted before long.

"Hi guys, welcome to Champion Recruiters!"

A caffeine-riddled brunette woman burst into the room carrying all manner of papers and files and dropped them down onto the table at the head of the room.

"Good to see you all again, how are we all feeling this morning?"

Lindsey said “fine”. The other girl said “great”. The guy just nodded his head again.

“Awesome, I bet you can’t wait to get started.”

This was Jane, the head of HR at Champion Recruiters and one of the people who had been present at Lindsey’s interview a week earlier. She seemed a friendly enough woman, if a little tightly wound, but it was at least a relief to have some life injected into the room.

“I know first days are always hard, but I promise to make this as painless as possible for you. If I can start by getting you all to sign your induction form.”

She handed each of them a sheet of paper. Lindsey looked down at it and saw it was a letterhead emblazed with the company logo and its motto: ‘We hire the best for the best’.

How inspirational.

Lindsey wasn’t sure that she considered herself to be the best at anything, certainly not anything to do with being gainfully employed. This was to be her first ‘proper’ job, a step up from the part-time work she had done to get her through her younger days when she just needed a bit of extra cash to pay for fun things like partying and holidays. Most of what she earnt now would disappear on rent and utility bills and, by the looks of things, on some kind of professional business attire.

If she did have to be the best at something, she wouldn’t have picked being a recruitment consultant. She would have preferred to be the best traveller, or the best blogger, or the best at avoiding ever having to get a proper job at all.

She sighed and signed her name on the dotted line at the bottom of the page before sliding it back across the table for Jane to collect.

"Thanks guys. Now usually Ali, our company founder, would pop in and introduce himself to you all, but he's had to go on an urgent business trip to Paris this morning so unfortunately, he won't be here. But I'm sure he will check in with you later in the week."

Lindsey knew who she was referring to, having browsed the company's website in preparation for her interviews. Ali was the founder of Champion Recruiters, and his bio was a lengthy and well-edited page on the website. The type of language used in the bio was brash, confident and self-serving and if Lindsey had to guess, she'd say that Ali had written it himself. From what she had read, it was clear that he was a classic salesman, a trait which had obviously equipped him to achieve great things in the world of recruitment. How far her own lack of sales skills would get her in the same ruthless world remained to be seen.

She had been surprised to receive a job offer from Champion, considering she had no previous experience or contacts in the industry. Her application had been more out of desperation to pay for her future life in London than of any real desire to work as a recruiter. But the interview had gone well, despite all her waffling, and she had been assured that success in the job was less about experience and more about confidence and having a 'can do' attitude. At times it had even felt like they were trying to sell her on the job more than she was trying to sell them on her. But she had told them that she possessed the confidence required. She just hadn't added the bit about her confidence only usually emerging after a bottle of wine or a good session on a sunbed. Although her confidence had been given a more natural boost by what had happened to her on her train journey into the office today.

As Jane stood at the head of the room and began to talk through a series of dry PowerPoint slides, Lindsey thought about the guy who she had met on the tube this morning. She had just given up her seat for an elderly gentleman when she had noticed a handsome young man staring at her from the aisle. She wouldn't have given him a second look were it not for his great eyes and the fact that he was wearing a beanie hat, which seemed a little unusual, considering the weather.

She had self-consciously lowered her eyes back to her phone screen but couldn't help noticing that he was moving closer to her. Either he was going to charm her with a smooth opening line, or he was going to confirm that he was a bit of a weirdo and that the hat was just the tip of the iceberg. She had held her breath and prayed for the former.

"Hi," he had said simply, flashing her a smile and looking at her with his deep blue eyes.

It was so simple, so ordinary, yet that one word was enough to make her smile, and from there, the conversation had begun.

Lindsey had often wondered why more men didn't approach women in a simple way. *What was the need for cheesy chat-up lines or bad jokes when often a simple hello would do the trick?* But this guy in the beanie hat had kept it simple, and she appreciated that.

After a little bit of chit chat about how busy the tube was and how he wasn't a fan of Monday mornings, Lindsey had been relieved to see that he wasn't a weirdo. That instantly moved him ahead of the last three guys who had tried to chat her up over the past week. But she had still been intrigued about the beanie hat on his head. The guy must have been boiling under there. But she would never ask. Too afraid to be rude. And she didn't want to say anything that might ruin the first good pick-up attempt she had experienced in a long time.

But then the man had asked for her number, and she had seen an opportunity.

"I'll give you my number if you tell me why you are wearing a winter hat in summer," she had replied with a smile.

He had laughed and joked that he got asked that question a lot, before quickly clarifying that it didn't mean he chatted up girls every day on the tube. Lindsey had laughed and been surprised at how comfortable she already felt in his presence. Then he had finally told her the reason for the hat. A bad haircut. Dodgy barber. The worst, apparently. She had burst out laughing again and asked to see the haircut so she could judge for herself, but he had playfully refused. She had fulfilled her end of the bargain and given him her phone number just as the train arrived at her stop.

They had departed with a goodbye and a smile and the promise that he would text her shortly. The whole encounter had made her feel good and was the main reason why she had walked into the office for her first day at Champion Recruiters without any nerves or anxiety. She wasn't looking for a boyfriend. But a bit of fun with a good-looking and cheeky guy she had met on the tube?

Why not?

Lindsey suddenly realised that Jane was moving onto the fifth slide in her presentation and that she hadn't listened to a word of it so far. The other two inductees were furiously scribbling in the notebooks they had brought with them as part of their professional preparation for today.

Lindsey didn't even have a pen, never mind a notebook.

She quickly looked around for something that would make it look as if she were as engrossed in this presentation as the other two were, but there was nothing else in the room that she could use to write with. Then she had an idea.

"Sorry," she said, interrupting Jane who was mid-flow, talking about something to do with exponential growth and client satisfaction. *"Is it okay if I make some notes on my phone? I find it easier to keep track that way rather than writing them down."*

Jane thought for a moment before shrugging.

"I guess so. I suppose it's the modern way. I'm sure we won't even need paper and pens soon."

Lindsey smiled and took out her phone, also taking the opportunity to catch the eyes of the other inductees who now looked so old-fashioned and obsolete with their antiquated ways of note-taking. As Jane returned to her spiel, Lindsey noticed she had just received a text message from an unknown number, but she soon figured out who it was from by the content.

Hey, how's your morning going? I'm bored already. P.S. Do you know a good hairdresser?

Lindsey smiled. It was the guy from the train. She typed back her reply, safe in the knowledge that to Jane, it would just look like she was taking notes on her speech.

Mornings ok. Had better. Sorry can't help you on the haircut but I know a place you can buy a good hat she sent back.

She waited for the reply, a little too impatiently, she noted. But she was glad of the distraction, not only from the presentation but in general. Life was always more fun when there was a love interest on the scene. She soon had another message.

What's wrong with the hat I already have?

Lindsey smiled again and typed her response.

Nothing. My grandad has one just like it.

She smirked at her own joke as she pressed send and looked back up at Jane, forcing herself to keep her eyes on the woman until she felt her phone vibrate in her hand again. Another message. This was going well.

Haha, I see we have a comedian amongst us. Does she have a name?

Lindsey suddenly realised then that amongst all the chatting and the flirting on the train and over text they hadn't actually formally introduced themselves.

Best comedian in London she replied. ***I'm Lindsey by the way. And you are...***

She sent the message then waited. What was his name? James maybe? A Richard? Could be a Dan? Or even a Paul?

Nice to meet you Lindsey. I'm Diego.

Hmmm. That was unexpected, she thought. Diego? That sounded foreign, yet he had a London accent. The plot thickened...

She moved her gaze back to the presentation slides at the front of the room and thought about how random it was that she had met Diego on the train that morning. Commuting on public transport was obviously rubbish, yet there was no doubt it offered opportunities to interact with others. Most of the interactions would be negative. Pushing and shoving. Sighing and tutting. But some of them could be positive.

She suddenly remembered the old woman she had seen on the same train with the handbag and the expensive rings. The tears she had tried to conceal. Lindsey wondered again what had caused the emotional response from the stranger. She also wondered where she was now. Hopefully feeling better.

But she would never know.

Carol

08:45

London City Hospital, Central London

Carol Heath already knew her fate. She didn't need a doctor to confirm it. The news would be bad. Cancer. Terminal. Months to live. Make your preparations. Say your goodbyes.

Slip away into the darkness...

The chair she was sitting on in the busy waiting room was uncomfortable. It was a completely insignificant thing to notice at that moment in time, yet it was somehow reassuring. She was grateful for the chair, even if it was hard and unkind on her fifty-nine-year-old bones. She was grateful for all the people around her, sitting on identical chairs and waiting for their own appointments with their own doctors. Most of all, she was grateful for life because soon it would be over and there was nothing she could do about it.

Now she was in this mindset she was surprised to notice how she wasn't thinking about all the good things she was going to miss. She was actually thinking about all the little things that used to annoy her but now made her smile because she was still alive to witness them. Like the tube journey to the hospital this morning. Usually, she hated being crammed into a carriage with a bunch of rude commuters who never gave her enough personal space. But she had savoured every minute of it today. Every passenger. Every stop.

Every second.

Like the young boy who had been running around the waiting room ever since she had got here fifteen minutes ago, shouting loudly and bumping into the back of her chair. Ordinarily, she would be irritated that the boy's parents weren't calming him down and teaching him how to behave appropriately in public. But today she just smiled at the boy, enjoying his exuberance and youthful ways. And she wasn't even annoyed that, so far, her appointment was running five minutes behind schedule. What used to be frustrating was now welcome. Every minute that passed wasn't a minute of delay.

It was a minute of life.

She knew that, in time, she would start to dwell on all the things that she would miss out on when she was gone. Like retirement with her husband, Steve. Lunch dates with her daughter, Francesca. And playdates with her grandson Jack. But for now, she was just appreciating the world for what it was. And there was nowhere that made you more conscious of how insignificant we all are more than a hospital waiting room, surrounded by fellow patients all thinking the same thing.

Am I going to die?

Carol looked at the woman sitting opposite her. It was hard to tell her age, but she was much younger than her. Very skinny. Very still. She was lost in the book she was reading. A Paula Hawkins novel. Carol hadn't read that one, but it had been on her to-do list. Like the million other things that wouldn't get done now. The woman with the book didn't seem at all perturbed by the screaming child or the busy room or the delays in the appointment system. Just like Carol, she seemed content with her lot. Happy to take her time. Happy simply to have time.

The bandana on the young woman's head was a dark shade of blue and covered her whole scalp. Her lack of eyebrows suggested that the woman was probably bald. Carol wondered how much chemotherapy the woman had been through. Was she halfway through a cycle? At the end of it? Maybe she was here today to learn if it had made any impact on the horrible disease that was ravaging her body. Hopefully it would be good news, but it was probably just as likely to be bad.

Like Carol's.

She wondered how the woman in the bandana had taken it when she had first been diagnosed with cancer. Had she been shocked, or had she been expecting it? Did she cry or simply shrug? Ask questions or take it as it came? Carol thought about how she was going to respond to her diagnosis when it was given to her in a few moments' time. It was hard to predict exactly how she would feel when the words were delivered to her by a medical professional, but she was determined to take it positively. No crying. No self-pity. No pleading for the doctor to save her. She would nod. She would smile. She would thank the doctor and tell him that she was ready to begin whatever course of treatment he prescribed. Then she would stand up straight and tall and walk out of the room with her head held high. She would leave the hospital and walk back to the train station. She would board the train to take her home. And when she got there, she would load the washing machine and tidy the kitchen and prepare the casserole that she and Steve would enjoy when he got home from work later that evening. Everything would carry on as normal, because life went on.

That was all there was to it.

She would have to break the news to her family, of course. She would tell Steve first, probably tonight after the casserole and a glass of red wine had taken the edge off the events of the day. She would deliver the news in a straightforward manner, being realistic but optimistic at the same time. He would be upset. He was an emotional man. That's why she loved him. But she would reassure him that everything would be alright. They would face the challenge of her chemotherapy together and whatever the outcome, they had been lucky to enjoy many happy years together. At some point down the line, when the cancer had really taken hold of her, she would take his hand as he sat by her bedside and she would tell him that she wanted him to find somebody else after she had gone. He deserved to love again. To have somebody with whom to share his retirement. She wouldn't want him to feel like he was betraying her memory. She just wanted him to be happy.

After she had told her husband, she would have to tell her daughter, Francesca, and Francesca's husband, David. Francesca would cry; there was no doubt about that. She would take the news the worst. She would get angry.

At the cancer. At the doctors. At the world.

She would weep into Carol's shoulder. Then David would take over and perform his husbandly duties until she pulled herself together. Then she would be on the internet, reading and researching breast cancer and all the best ways to beat it. Wonder drugs. Herbal remedies. Miracle cures. Because Francesca was like that. Always seeking answers, even in places where there weren't any to be found.

Then there was her grandson, Jack. He was only six years old, so there was a limit to how much he would understand about his grandma's illness. But he would pick up on how upset his mummy was and how Grandma seemed to be going bald and getting thinner and losing her energy quicker during their playtimes. So they would have to tell him. Grandma was poorly. She was being looked after by the doctors and nurses. She was being given special medicine. Being the sweet little boy that he was, he would try to help her himself. He would play the role of doctor and bring her his own version of medicine in a little cup. Carol would take the sweets from it and eat them all, telling him that she already felt better for taking them. He would flush with pride and go back for more medicine, happy that he was helping his granny get better and performing an important duty within the family.

She would also have to break the news to her friends, both her oldest ones and her work colleagues. They would rally around her and try to take her mind off her fate with multiple social events to fill her calendar. Lunches. Tickets to the theatre. Weekend walks. They would keep her spirits lifted and also support Steve, whom they all knew so well and adored.

It wouldn't be so bad. She had a great network around her. They would make whatever time she had left more special. Not everybody was lucky enough to have family and friends like hers, so she was in no position to be ungrateful. She wouldn't have swapped her life for the world. Her fate was her fate, and everything that had come before had been leading up to this very moment.

"Carol Heath."

She looked up at the doctor standing in one of the two doorways to the waiting room. His name was Dr Mukesh, and she had seen him once before when he had examined her and recommended that she have a scan after an initial referral from her usual GP, Dr Hayes. He was a small man, no taller than 5'7, and he looked well for his age, which Carol guessed to be around the forty mark. His black hair was trimmed short, and his white shirt was crease-free and pristine. And he had a nice manner about him as all good medical professionals should. He had put her at ease when he had first seen her, and he was putting her at ease now with the warm and welcoming smile that he gave her as she made her way across the room towards him.

"Hi, follow me," he said, leading Carol to the room where she would be given the news of her disease.

She followed Dr Mukesh, clutching her handbag and making sure not to let the coat that was draped over her arm drag along the floor.

It was the same room she had been in before when she had talked through her symptoms and then removed the top half of her clothing for him to have a look. She hadn't been embarrassed about the fact she had been standing topless in front of a stranger. The fear of what he might find had overpowered any shyness or self-consciousness about her aging, plump body. And besides, he probably examined a dozen women a day. There was nothing special about her. To him, she was just another person with an illness. One of those statistics in the adverts. The one out of every two people who would get cancer in their lifetime.

"Take a seat," said Dr Mukesh. He walked around his large desk to the swivel chair positioned in front of the window. The view was largely obscured by thin grey blinds, but that didn't matter. There didn't seem to be anything particular to see outside, just some non-descript buildings and the blue sky above. Dr Mukesh probably didn't have much need for a nice view anyway. He had more important things to think about.

Responsibilities to his patients. Enhancing his knowledge of the medical world.

And trying to keep a blank face when he told someone that they were going to die.

Carol put her coat and handbag down on the spare seat, then slowly settled her body into the chair and faced the polite Indian man with the gentle manner.

"So how have you been?" he asked her, obviously deciding that a slow and subtle approach was the best way to proceed.

"Okay," Carol replied, downplaying the rollercoaster of emotions she had been on ever since she had discovered a lump in her breast whilst showering two weeks earlier.

"Good. Well I won't waste any more time. I have the results of your scan here."

Dr Mukesh clicked on the mouse that was connected to his desktop computer, and Carol watched his eyes dart about as he observed the image he had brought up on screen. She didn't need to see it to know what it showed. A dark spot. A tumour. Cancer. She'd seen enough images of bad news scans online during the past few weeks, so she just kept her eyes on the doctor's unreadable face and waited for him to confirm what she already knew.

"I'm pleased to say that we found absolutely nothing of concern," he said calmly, looking away from the screen at the woman in front of him. *"The scan was clear."*

Carol's heart almost leapt out of her chest. *What did he just say?*

"Excuse me?" she replied when she finally felt the power of speech return to her.

"The lump you felt is nothing to worry about. Just a benign cyst. Have a look."

He turned the computer screen so she could see the X-ray. It was all clear. No dark spots. No tumours. *No cancer.*

"Now we can remove the cyst if it's causing you discomfort, but if not, then there is no need to touch it. There is nothing in it that would cause me any concern, but it's entirely up to you."

He smiled at her again, but she was still too busy staring at the inside of her body on the computer screen to notice. He really was telling her that there was nothing wrong with her. She was healthy. She was going to live a long life. It was all over as quickly as a bad dream.

"Okay," she said, all other words failing her.

Because it was okay. Everything was going to be okay. She was going to be okay.

"Okay you want to leave it, or okay you want it removed?"

She finally pulled her gaze from the screen and looked at the doctor who was leaning forward in his chair towards her.

"Okay, I'll leave it."

Dr Mukesh nodded his head and turned the screen back to face him.

"No problem, you can always change your mind in future if it gets any bigger, but I don't imagine that it will and as I said, it's nothing to worry about if it does."

Carol nodded. It was all so simple and straightforward.

Would it have been the same if it had been cancer? Would he be sitting there all confident and composed if he had just told her she had six months to live? Would she be sitting there all relaxed and presentable, or would she be rolling around on the floor in hysterics and screaming at the world about how cruel life had been to her?

She would never know. Because it was good news. Now all that was left was to walk away and go back to her life. Like nothing had ever happened. Except of course it had.

As she thanked Dr Mukesh and left his office, she knew the experience of the last few weeks would stay with her forever. After all, nothing could have made her press the pause button on life more quickly than such a terrifying health scare. Just like nothing would get her to press the restart button more quickly than getting the all-clear.

Life begins at fifty-nine Carol thought to herself as she made her way back through the waiting room, past the young woman in the blue bandana and towards the sliding glass doors that would put her back onto the busy streets of Central London.

Life begins now.

Farooq

08:46

Central London

Farooq Baq really wished the person sitting in the back of his car had called an ambulance instead of a taxi. Now, instead of it being the responsibility of the paramedics to get the ailing patient to hospital in time, it was his. But he was just an Uber driver.

And a tired one at that.

"Can you wind the window down?" the woman on the backseat of his Prius breathlessly begged him between her deep and dramatic inhalations of air.

He quickly complied, not sure how helpful a hit of London air would be for a woman in labour, but happy to do it if it meant she stopped panicking for a moment.

He knew he was only a minute away from the hospital but judging by the noises behind him, he knew that even that might not be sufficient time. Visions of having to try and deliver the baby by the roadside himself were enough to make him put his foot down a little harder on the accelerator.

Thankfully the traffic was relatively light; some of the inner city streets were closed to all vehicles except emergency teams, buses and taxis, as a trial to reduce the capital's carbon footprint. If this had been a normal day, with normal levels of traffic, the woman would have stood no chance of making it to the hospital in time. Her baby would have come into the world in a taxi, by the hands of a bewildered and terrified Indian man.

Baby Prius.

How cute.

But Farooq was aware that even with the favourable traffic conditions it was touch and go as to whether he was going to make it to the front door of the A & E department in time to hand his passenger over to much more capable hands than his own.

He looked in his rear-view mirror and saw the woman leaning out of the window, sucking in deep mouthfuls of the early morning air. He considered that perhaps gulping in highly-polluted London air wouldn't be particularly beneficial to her unborn child but thought it best not to mention that to her. She had enough on her mind. Like worrying that the first thing her baby would see would be an Indian man throwing up by the roadside after being required to cut the umbilical cord.

Farooq felt a little queasy himself now and put down his own window, taking his opportunity to get a hit of the smoggy air into his lungs. As he did, he thought about how he could easily have been on his way home right now to a nice breakfast and a lie down instead of racing across London on a medical mission. Having completed a series of lucrative early morning jobs while many of his competitors slept, he had been debating whether to call it a day. There had been an airport run to Heathrow to drop off a businessman. There had been a long trip across the city from Vauxhall to Enfield to drop off a young lady who looked as if she'd spent an impromptu night at a new acquaintance's house. And there had been plenty of smaller fares to keep him busy. They had all added up to a good night's work, and he had been so close to calling it quits and going home to his flat in South London. But then he had seen a fare request pop up on his phone from a woman called Bethany and, being only two minutes away from her location, he had decided to grab a little more cash while he could.

But however much he stood to make from this fare paled into insignificance when compared to the mental stress of having to deliver a pregnant woman to a hospital in a race against the clock.

When he had arrived at Bethany's location, he had found her standing on the street, almost bent double in pain and clutching a large pink sports bag that looked full to the brim. He had initially been concerned that she was hurt and had grabbed her possessions as she fled from someone potentially dangerous, so he had jumped out of his seat as soon as he was parked and gone to her assistance. But it had quickly become apparent that she hadn't been injured, nor was she trying to get away from someone.

She just needed to get somewhere and fast.

"I'm having a baby" she had shouted at him as he had fussed around her and tried to calm her down.

He had immediately pulled open the back passenger door and watched as she struggled in pain to fit her swollen, baby-carrying body into his vehicle. Then he had been straight back behind the wheel and on his way, barely having time to close his door as he accelerated to the speed limit.

Conversation had unsurprisingly been at a minimum for the majority of the journey up to this present point, barring some explicit swear words and world-class backseat driving.

"HURRY UP!"

"GO AROUND HIM!"

"PUT YOUR FOOT DOWN!"

Farooq hadn't been under this much pressure since he had taken his very first driving test back in India almost twenty years earlier. He had been a taxi driver ever since he had earned his driver's licence, firstly for six years in his home city of Mumbai and then for fourteen years in London after he and his wife had made the move back in the ninetie's. They had left their home country for a better life and had generally managed to find one in the time they had been over here. He was a forty-one-year-old UK resident with a wife working in the NHS and two children attending a good college in the capital. He couldn't complain, though he would complain if Bethany kicked the back of his chair one more time.

"Are you okay?" he asked her politely, trying to stay calm as he neared the hospital.

"What do you think?" she screamed back at him, and he decided that he wouldn't ask her any more questions from now on.

He really wished his wife was here. She was a nurse, and though not a midwife, she would know what to do to handle the situation. She would know the right things to say and the right course of action to take in order to give Bethany the best possible outcome. All Farooq could do was keep pushing on his vehicle's accelerator and hope for the best.

But as he reached a bend in the road, he had no choice but to slow down and eat up precious seconds that might make the difference between Bethany making it to the hospital in time or not. But as the car turned onto the next street, he saw the blue flashing lights of an ambulance up ahead and knew he was almost there.

"Ten more seconds!" he shouted but, glancing in the rear-view mirror, he saw that Bethany probably hadn't heard him.

She had her eyes squeezed shut and was clutching her stomach whilst making a loud, guttural sound that Farooq had only previously heard on television in episodes of Casualty. He didn't know much about medicine, or the process of childbirth, but he figured by the severity of the sound that time was almost up. The baby was probably crowning. Best case scenario now was that it would be delivered on the doorstep of the hospital.

Worst case scenario, he would suddenly have an extra passenger in his car.

Could he charge extra for that? Somehow, he seriously doubted that would go down well with the exhausted mother on his backseat.

He guessed that Bethany was in her mid-twenties and he could tell that she was probably a good-looking young woman when she was in her normal state of presentation. Unfortunately, right now her hair was a sweaty, tangled mess and her face was a twisted knot of agony so it was hard to tell what she really looked like when she wasn't going through the most painful thing a woman can experience.

When he had first started the journey, he had wondered if there was somebody who should be with her at the hospital. A partner. Or a parent. They would undoubtedly miss the birth itself, but he hoped whoever it was would be there soon after to give the exhausted woman some much-needed support and share with her the joy of her newborn child.

Farooq remembered how he had felt during the births of his own two children, Iqbal and Eva. Becoming a father had been the most magical experience of his life. And the most petrifying. His wife had been strong, brave and brilliant through both of the deliveries. But she had also been wild, possessed, and intimidating as he had stood beside her and held her hand.

He had never felt so useless as he did back then, standing by and merely watching as his wife did all the pushing and the nurses did all the delivering. Until today. He felt the same uselessness right now, although at least he was playing a part in getting the woman to where she needed to be.

He saw the ambulance make a left turn up ahead into the hospital grounds.

"Okay we're almost there," he told Bethany, though he doubted she could hear him amidst all the noise she was making whilst trying to delay her baby's arrival.

He slowed down, turned left and passed through the entrance that would lead him directly to the Accident & Emergency department. He had never been to this particular hospital before, but he did have experience when it came to visiting A & E. When his son Iqbal had been seven, he had accidentally swallowed a piece of plastic that had broken off one of his toys and the faulty part had become lodged in his throat. With his young boy turning blue, and the Heimlich manoeuvre not helping the situation, his wife had frantically called 999. But Farooq had been unable simply to wait for rescue to arrive and so he had scooped his poorly boy in his arms and run to his car.

While his wife and daughter had done their best to keep Iqbal calm on the backseat, Farooq had raced through the streets of London, which had thankfully been relatively quiet because it had been almost 8 o'clock in the evening. He had paid no regard to speed limit or road safety at the time, because who would when their child was struggling to breathe? Within ten minutes, he had been able to deliver his stricken child to the hospital, and they had worked amazingly quickly to dislodge the piece of plastic that had caused so much distress.

Farooq had often wondered what would have happened if he hadn't taken the decision to get his son to hospital himself that night. Would the ambulance have been quicker? Could he have made the situation worse by taking him himself? Or had he actually saved his boy's life by taking decisive action and not just waiting for the paramedics to arrive? He would never be sure how things would have played out if he had waited. Maybe it would have been fine. Maybe he would have lost him. All he knew was that Iqbal was taking his A-Levels right now and planning on becoming a lawyer. Most importantly, he was a healthy young man. That was all that mattered.

Just like all that mattered now was that the woman in his backseat was given the best possible chance to give birth to her own precious child safely.

He parked behind the ambulance and leapt out of his seat, running around the car and opening the door that Bethany was curled up by.

Realising she was in far too much pain to leave the vehicle, he looked around for assistance and saw a security guard standing outside the door to the emergency department smoking a cigarette and looking at his phone.

"Hey you! Help!" he shouted to the man, who dropped his cigarette to the floor when he saw the agonised woman in the back of the Prius and the crazy Indian man leaping about beside her.

The security guard quickly ran through the sliding doors to the hospital, and within seconds he was back, this time followed by two paramedics who he must have found somewhere in the reception area.

Upon seeing the arrival of the medical professionals, Farooq felt the same sense of relief that he had felt when he had carried his son into A & E all those years ago. Bethany would be in good hands now, just like Iqbal had been in.

He stood to one side while the two paramedics quickly examined the patient decided how to proceed.

One of them shouted for someone to get a wheelchair. Another told him they might have to deliver the baby right there, in the car.

It seemed silly, but when he heard that, Farooq thought about what it might mean for the inside of his taxi. After all, it was his livelihood. Somehow the £100 soiling charge sticker he had in his back window didn't seem like it would cover it. But that was just his brain's way of trying to make light of a crazy situation.

As a nurse raced out of the building, pushing a wheelchair in front of her, Farooq thought about how he would tell this story to his family later that day. His children would be amazed that their father had been caught up in such drama. His wife would be proud of him and maybe even call him a hero. And maybe one day Bethany would tell her child about the day he or she was born and the nice Indian man who had driven her to the hospital as she was giving birth.

He watched Bethany being pushed towards the hospital doors in a wheelchair, relieved that this story would seemingly have a happy ending. He also felt relieved that his Prius wouldn't have to be listed as the baby's place of birth.

London City Hospital would look a lot better on the birth certificate form than Mr Baq's Prius, RW2 71F, that was sure.

Bogdan

08:47

London City Hospital, Central London

Bogdan Petrovic knew his life would never be the same again. The chance encounter with Jelena in the London Underground had changed everything. Before that, he had just been a lonely man working long hours in a dead-end job, with few goals and little direction in his life. But now things were different. Regardless of what happened with Jelena and whether she wanted to see him again or not, he had a new purpose. He was going to find the men that were responsible for the abuse and torture inflicted upon the woman from his home country, and he was going to make them pay. No matter how many were involved, no matter how large the operation was, he was going to have his revenge - for Jelena and for every other woman who had fallen victim to them. He had no idea where to begin, and he had no idea if it was even possible, but he knew that he couldn't simply go back to his previous life. He had been sleepwalking before today.

But now he was awake.

Of course, whatever happened in the future, most of all, he hoped that Jelena would want to see him again. It was hard to tell because she couldn't speak the words, but the way she had squeezed his hand in the ambulance and looked at him as the nurses had wheeled her away down the hospital corridor had told him that she needed him just as much as he needed her.

He would stay in this waiting room until the medical professionals had finished helping her, and she was in a more stable condition. If she wanted him to leave then, if she never wanted to see him again, then he would accept it. He would have no choice. It would be understandable if she didn't. His face may always remind her of this time in her life, a time when she had been afraid and broken. But his face may also be a reminder of her rescue, and her newfound hope and freedom.

He prayed it was the latter.

It had been a miracle for both of them that they had found each other when they had, on the escalators beneath Euston Station. He had saved her from a life of torment and pain, and she had inadvertently saved him from a life of solitude and waste.

While Jelena's situation had been entirely against her will, his had been self-inflicted. He had always thought that moving to England and finding work would solve all his problems. But of course, it hadn't. He had still been the same person. He still had the same needs as anyone else. Comfort. Control. Companionship. And he had been lacking in all those things, no matter how much he tried to convince himself he wasn't. Just because you have money, it doesn't mean you are well off. Just because you have a job, it doesn't mean you have a say. And just because you are surrounded by millions of people every day, it doesn't mean you aren't lonely.

Bogdan looked at the clock on the wall above the reception desk and saw that it was approaching nine in the morning. Usually, he would be asleep now, his exhausted body stretched out in his one-bedroom flat, getting some rest before beginning another night of double-shift cleaning duties. Instead, he was sitting upright in a plastic chair that only just contained his broad, bulky body and feeling more awake than he had done in a long time. He didn't know how long he would have to wait here before he knew that Jelena was okay, but he knew one thing. He would wait as long as it took.

He had tried to get some answers from the nurses about the nature of her injuries and what they were going to do to her, but they had told him nothing. Having established that he wasn't family, they had refused to tell him any more until they had stabilised Jelena and contacted her next of kin. He knew that would take a while, on both counts. Her relatives were presumably back in Serbia and reaching them might be difficult, if not impossible. And stabilising her would be even tougher, if not physically, then certainly mentally. It was clear she was severely malnourished, but hopefully, an IV drip and the steady introduction of proper food would resolve that. The area where they had cut out her tongue was likely to be infected, or at least extremely painful, and work would need to be done there to clean the wound and reduce her discomfort. And there were likely to be bruised bones and sprained ligaments from all the beatings she had taken at the hands of her captors, which would only heal with time and due care and attention.

But most of all, it was her mental state that needed stabilising.

He couldn't even begin to imagine what was going on in her head right now and all that had gone before it. She had probably been through some of the worst experiences a human being could be subjected to, and even though she was safe now the torture would never really end. Not completely. There would be nightmares, flashbacks, and panic attacks. Jumping at shadows. A fear of dark rooms. A fear of other men. Maybe even a fear of him, despite him being her rescuer. Then there was the permanent damage to her body. The years it may have taken off her life. The disabilities she would have to live with now. The fact that she would never be able to speak clearly again.

She would have to be incredibly strong to get through the next few days and weeks and almost as strong to build a new life for herself after all that. He wondered if he would have the strength to meet those challenges and was afraid to say that he couldn't be sure. There was likely to be a lot of depression and anxiety in her life now, which would rob her of being the person she was before all this.

The person he had known from his school classes back in Serbia.

He recalled that Jelena had always been one of the brightest pupils in the class. Bogdan himself, not so much. While she had spent most of the lessons answering the teacher's questions and scribbling notes into her books, he was often found at the back of the classroom doodling on the desks and daydreaming about growing up and getting out of there. She had been a happy girl, always smiling and laughing with her friends, of which there were many. She was also popular with the other boys in her class, her long dark hair and her energetic personality a powerful combination for teenage boys to try and resist. Bogdan had been one of many who had fallen under her spell, but he was also one of many who had never acted on their feelings. He had never thought much of his chances anyway, what with her being so pretty and him being so podgy.

Although much of his pubescent puppy fat had turned into muscle as he'd grown older, he had still been just one of many desperate boys vying for the attention of the females in their class and, like most of them, he hadn't had any success. But that hadn't stopped him from dreaming about how things would be different once he had grown up and left school.

Of course, life hadn't turned out exactly as he had hoped. His dreams of a powerful and lucrative career in the business world had been shot down by the poor grades he had achieved in his final exams, so he embarked on a journey of exhausting and poorly-paid manual jobs to get him to this point in his twenty-nine-year-old life. He couldn't complain. He had his health, just about, although his back kept him awake most nights due to all the bending and heavy lifting he had subjected it to over the years. But as he got older, he realised that money wasn't the magical solution it had seemed to be when he was sitting in his classroom dreaming about it. True wealth, he had come to appreciate as he had observed other people on trains or in parks, was measured by who you shared your life with. A wife or a husband. A son or a daughter. A best friend. That was all you really needed to be happy. Long before moving to England, Bogdan had become painfully aware that he didn't have any of those things, and that he wouldn't be truly happy until he did. No matter how many extra shifts he worked as a cleaner, or how much he tried to save while renting the cheapest, grottiest flat he could find. He needed someone in his life to share things with. And now, maybe, he would have that with Jelena.

At worst, he hoped they could be friends. Take walks together. Visit a tourist attraction. Laugh about their school days in Belgrade. But at best, maybe they could be something more. Hold hands. Share a kiss. Lie together and fall asleep to the sounds of each other's breathing.

Because the truth was that he had never stopped loving her. Not since he had first laid eyes on her on the first day of secondary school as an eleven-year-old. Not since he had been largely ignored by her during all their classes together. Not since they had left school and gone off to make something of themselves in the world. Not since he had followed her on social media and liked some of the photos of her and her friends. Not since she had stopped posting updates online and disappeared entirely four months ago. And certainly not since he had encountered her in the train station that morning, 1,300 miles away from where he had last properly laid eyes on her as she waltzed away through the school gates, excited about what adult life had in store for her.

Now she was back in his life, and as much as he needed somebody, she needed somebody more. She had been to hell and back, and he could only begin to imagine most of it. It was likely he would never know the full extent of what she had been through. Maybe it was best that he didn't. But maybe she would share details with him. Maybe she would confide in him and seek comfort in his arms. Maybe they could get through this together and just maybe something truly amazing could come out of all this.

He was snapped out of his fantasy by the sight of two figures, one male, one female, approaching the reception desk. They wore plain clothes but, unlike everyone else in here, they didn't seem to be either seeking medical help or one of the employees of the hospital. They were more formal. Focused. And when he saw them take the badges out of their pockets and show them to the woman behind the desk, he knew who they were.

Detectives.

They were here for Jelena, and even though they were just doing their job, he felt protective of her and didn't want her forced into talking to them until she was fit and ready. He stood up and made his way over to them, and to where the woman behind the desk was pointing down the corridor towards the room in which Jelena was being treated.

"Excuse me," he said to the two detectives with the stern expressions and weary postures.

They both looked him up and down before the female spoke.

"Yes?" she replied bluntly.

"My name is Bogdan Petrovic, and I am the man who found Jelena," he told her, feeling a little prideful as he said it.

"You're the man from the station?" the male detective asked next and Bogdan nodded.

Just as he was about to tell them that Jelena needed rest before they bombarded her with their enquiries, they were interrupted by a female doctor approaching them.

"Excuse me, Mr Petrovic?" she enquired, looking at Bogdan through her weary eyes.

"Yes?" he replied, feeling his whole body tighten at the prospect of news on the patient she had been treating. *"How's Jelena? Is she okay?"*

The doctor smiled a little and put him at ease.

"She's doing well. We've given her something to ease her mental state, and although she's clearly been through a lot, she is going to get better with plenty of rest and rehabilitation."

Bogdan felt the relief flooding through his muscles and allowed himself to breathe once again.

"Detective Rose. This is Detective Taylor. We would like to speak to the patient if that's okay with you" the female detective said to the doctor.

Before Bogdan could interject with his own concerns, he was glad to hear the doctor's voice reject the request.

"Of course, but at the moment I can't allow that. She's been through a terrible ordeal and is quite heavily sedated. I'm afraid any questioning will have to wait a little longer until I am sure she is in a more stable mental condition than she is currently."

The detectives were clearly not pleased to hear this and were just about to protest when the doctor turned back to Bogdan and smiled again.

"She wrote something just before we put her under. She wanted me to give it to you."

Bogdan looked down to see a small folded piece of paper being put into his hand. The doctor smiled again at him, then turned and walked away, quickly followed by the two detectives who still were doing their best to get to the patient.

But Bogdan left them to it and instead returned to his seat in the busy waiting room. Once he was sitting down, he slowly unfolded the piece of paper and saw the same scraggly handwriting as he had seen in the back of the ambulance only twenty minutes earlier.

It took him a couple of read-throughs to understand what it said, but when he got it, a large smile spread across his face.

Thank you for saving me.

Please wait for me.

Jelena x

Next in the 20 Minute Series...

20 Minutes In The Park

Set one month later, several characters will return, alongside many new ones, on a busy Sunday afternoon in Hyde Park, London, where there is much more than just the sounds of nature in the air.

There's the threat from the mysterious murderer roaming the footpaths. There's the music from the festival where a recently released criminal is about to unleash havoc. And there's the chance at revenge for a heroic couple who never thought they would get it...

20 Minutes. 20 People. 20 reasons why this is more than just a walk in the park.

OUT NOW

Read on for a sneak peek at the next chapter...

Jelena

14:20

Jelena Markovic couldn't believe her eyes. She wanted them to be wrong. She wanted them not to see him. But it was clear to her now that the man walking across the park only metres away from her was the same man that had raped her earlier that year.

From her low vantage point, sitting on a blanket on the grass, he looked taller than she had remembered him. But he hadn't seen her sitting nearby and simply continued on his way like it was just another day.

His strides were short but quick, and his head bobbed a little as he moved. He wore a dark blue t-shirt and black jeans and dazzlingly white trainers that stood out even more as they moved from the concrete path and onto the lush green grass that surrounded it. But he wore one other item of clothing that was unusual for this time of year.

A grey beanie hat covering his hair and ears.

It was twenty-five-degrees in London today, and there was no need for a hat. But Jelena knew why he was wearing it.

She knew exactly what he was trying to cover up.

The man was dressed differently to the last time she had seen him, which had been just before he took his suit off and dominated her in that locked room. He had exuded money, power and a frightening sense of control that day. But he didn't exude any of those things today, especially not here in the open freedom of Hyde Park. Today he just looked like a normal guy in his thirties. Nobody else would have looked at him twice. But Jelena was still looking at him.

Because she knew who he really was.

It had now been a month since her ordeal at the hands of the Serbian sex traffickers had ended. After paying for a new life in the UK only to end up under lock and key and being used as a mere object for other people's pleasure, it had finally ended on that hot Monday morning on the London Underground in June. Since then she had done her best to regain a measure of control in her life that had been stripped from her during the horrific four-month experience, and while it was still an ongoing process, things had slowly been returning to something that resembled normality.

After receiving urgent medical treatment for the injuries and malnutrition she had endured in captivity, the first thing she had been made to do was deal with the British Police. Their questions had been extensive and exhaustive, and the experience of recalling every single detail from the crimes she had been victim to had left her feeling almost as empty as the real thing had.

The whole process had been made even more excruciating by the gravest of injuries she had sustained while living as a prisoner, which was that of the removal of her tongue. The medical staff at the hospital she had been taken too had been visibly appalled at what had been done to her, and while they did their best to clean the wounds and make her more comfortable, there had been nothing they could do to fix the issue of a vital piece of her body being taken from her.

It had taken some time until Jelena had been brave enough to look in the mirror and see the effects of the twisted surgery for the first time and understandably it had been a traumatic experience for her when she had. From a physical point of view, she had learnt to keep her mouth closed as much as she could when out in public which at least meant that other people had no idea what she was missing. But mentally, it was the knowledge that she now faced a lifetime of silence that had been the most difficult thing to process after the relief and euphoria of being rescued had subsided.

Of course, being unable to speak meant that dealing with the authorities' questions when they began had been problematic. Her only way of delivering her answers had been to type them on a laptop alongside the assistance of the Serbian translator who had been assigned to her case and while it was a successful process, it was also a long one. The task of communicating everything that had happened to her via a machine and an intermediary was both impersonal and longwinded, and it had taken all her considerable resolve to keep going until it was completed.

For the police, Jelena was something of a rare find. They explained how it was extremely unlikely that women like her that had been forced into sex work and held against their will ever actually escaped from that fate. While the officers in charge of her questioning weren't exactly excited by the chance to speak with her, they were at least a little overbearing. In terms of what she had been through, she was a victim, although in terms of the investigators, she was a prized possession.

But most of all, they had to remember that she was human.

She knew they were just trying to do their job, and more importantly stop it from happening to others like her, but that hadn't made the whole thing any easier. For several hours each day, beginning in the hospital and continuing in the shelter she was moved into once she was healing, she had answered as many questions as she could about what had happened.

She had described the two men who had taken her from the lorry in England and thrown her into the nightmarish existence that had never seemed likely to end. One of them tall, thin and pale, the other shorter, chubbier and meaner.

She told them how she had given them names, Volkov and Zao, and described in detail what each of them had done to her during their time together. She had explained how their threats of bringing harm to her surviving family members back home had kept her under their control until finally, she could take no more and had attempted her escape.

She told them how she had run through the underground only to be captured by Zao again and be dragged back towards the train. And finally, she had told them how the chance encounter with the man she had gone to school with had been the random factor that led to her ultimate rescue.

It hadn't been all one-way information, and the police had replied with facts of their own. Like how, after reviewing CCTV footage from the underground, they had been able to put a real name to one of the men that had taken Jelena.

Zao, the man that had been with her on the tube that morning, was in fact called Vukasin Dordevic. He was known to the authorities in Serbia and had spent time in prison for various combinations of theft, public indecency and drunken and disorderly behaviour. Quite how he had gone from partaking in petty crime to the more serious charges of sex trafficking and kidnapping was unclear, but one thing wasn't. He was a nasty piece of work and needed taking off the streets as soon as possible. Of course, Jelena had known that already and hoped that the information she had provided them would be enough to put a stop to his ruinous behaviour. But in the end, it had turned out somebody else had taken care of that.

When Jelena had taken the police back to the flat that she had been held in for so long, she had been shocked to see that it had been burnt to the ground. While the destruction of any evidence had been a severe blow to her, more was to follow. She was informed how the firefighting teams had discovered a body in the burnt-out flat, and after identification, it was revealed to be that of Vukasin.

The dead body of the old woman pulled out of the neighbouring flat posed even more of a mystery. But to Jelena, it was clear. The second man that had kidnapped her, the one she only knew by her given nickname of Volkov, was behind these despicable acts.

After taking care of evidence and witnesses, he had most likely returned to Serbia, and while the authorities there were on the lookout for him so far there had been no further updates. Just one CCTV image of him boarding the Eurostar train from Kings Cross to Paris on the morning that she escaped, wearing a blue cap pulled down tightly over his head and carrying a bag that she believed contained all the money he had been making from his crimes.

Without a real name to put to this mystery man's face Jelena knew deep down that it was highly unlikely he would ever be brought to justice, and she had forced herself to make some peace with that. The one thing she was struggling to make peace with though was the knowledge that it was likely there were other women out there going through the same thing she had been through and that she hadn't been able to help them.

Maybe if they had been able to catch her second kidnapper in the immediate aftermath of her escape, then they could have blown the lid off what was surely a larger network of sexual abuse and kidnapping crimes. But that hadn't been the case so far, and Jelena had expected she had helped the police as much as she could have done already.

Until she had seen the man walking through Hyde Park today just yards away from her.

He was one of the first men that she had been forced to be with during her time as a prisoner and he was the only man that she had been able to fight back against before he could do anything to her. With her legs and arms tied to the bed, it had been almost impossible to stop the man from being on top of her, and while she had begged for help and spat in his face, it had done little to dissuade him from what he wanted to do.

If he had kept his face above hers during the act, then there would have been no way to stop him. But at one point he had leaned down and attempted to bite Jelena on the neck, and that had been when she had taken the opportunity to sink her teeth into his left ear. She had tasted blood but refused to let go until she had torn off the upper part of the man's outer lobe. He had been shocked and screamed for help from the guards waiting outside as he held his hand up to the place where the blood poured from his head while Jelena had continued to spit at him and make noises of her own.

The beating that followed her act of defiance had been swift and brutal and hadn't done anything to stop the future attacks from taking place. But one good thing had come of it. She had never seen that man again.

Until today.

She kept her eyes on him and saw that he was heading for the large entrance gates that led into the music festival that was underway on the other side of the park. There weren't many parks in the world that could house a 10,000-capacity concert in one section while the rest of the space remained open to the public, but Hyde Park was one of them. It was a beautiful green space in the middle of the sprawling metropolis of London and Jelena had been doing her best to enjoy its features. But there were more urgent matters at hand now. She knew that if the man was to go through those gates and enter the crowds inside ,then she would never be able to find him again.

With that in mind, she rose quickly to her feet and set off in pursuit of him, leaving her blanket and shopping bag full of snacks behind her on the grass. She wasn't quite running, but it was a hurried jog, and she was forming her plan of action as she moved.

While she wouldn't be able to speak to the man herself, there was somebody else that she could get to do the talking. It was one of the security guards standing on the front gate of the festival, the guy wearing the bright green high visibility vest over his white shirt and black trousers. It would normally be too warm to wear such attire, but he was in uniform. It was her man.

It was Bogdan.

Ever since the pair of them had encountered each other in the London Underground that fateful day in June, they had grown closer. After he had called to her and distracted her captor enough for her to make a second and more successful escape she had leapt into his arms and held him so tightly he must have wondered if she was ever going to let go.

While they had not been particularly close while attending the same school in Belgrade in their childhood, they had been familiar enough with each other to recognise the other one despite it being over a decade since they had last spoken in person. The regular updating of photos to social platforms had helped them bridge the passage of time.

Jelena remembered Bogdan as the podgy, spotty boy from her classes although he had certainly changed. Much of the man's bulk now consisted of muscle instead of fat and the short buzz cut over his stubbly face had given him more of a handsome, rugged appearance than he had possessed in his youth.

He had visited her often while she was recovering in hospital, though he had made it clear he would have stopped doing so if she preferred solitude. He had been happy when she had told him that she would like to see him more after she had been released from care and even happier when she had taken his hand during one of their walks around the streets near her shelter.

They had continued to grow closer and while they hadn't yet been physical with each other, Jelena felt her feelings for him becoming stronger by the day.

After everything she had been through, she couldn't have imagined finding love in the same city where she had experienced nothing but evil and hatred. But she had, and she was glad she had stayed here.

Of course, there were other obstacles to overcome, and while communication was difficult between them, it wasn't impossible. She could write down her thoughts, and they were both in the process of learning sign language. They had even discussed potentially living together one day and her finding a job. When they had first reconnected, he had been working for a cleaning company but not long after that he had found a better-paid job working in security. It had led to him being assigned to Hyde Park today, to monitor and control the thousands of screaming music fans that had descended here for the festival.

Quickening her pace, Jelena saw the man ahead of her produce a ticket and show it to one of the inspectors on the turnstiles. Bogdan stood nearby, oblivious to the true nature of the person entering the premises that he was guarding, but she was only seconds away from telling him.

When Bogdan had told her that he would be working at Hyde Park today, she had decided on travelling with him. It was a nice day after all, and she felt it would be beneficial to her recovery to get some fresh air. Her plan had been to do a little sunbathing and walking in the park until Bogdan had finished his shift and they could travel back across London together.

That had been until she had seen the man that had abused her and now all plans were out the window.

Hers, Bogdan's and especially the man she was following.

She reached Bogdan just as the man in the grey beanie hat was passing through the ticket barriers. He still hadn't seen her, but by now Bogdan had, and the look of concern on his face told her she must be appearing frantic to him.

He asked her if everything was ok and she shook her head and pointed to the man walking into the festival. Before he had time to ask her what she meant, she had already taken out her mobile phone and typed her message on the screen.

Man in hat attacked me.

Then she touched her ear to let him know exactly which one he was. She had told Bogdan about the man whose flesh she had torn off with her teeth, and as soon as he read the message that she had typed out and seen the gesture towards her ear, then a look of realisation came across his face.

She nodded to signal how sure she was that it was him and that was all it took for Bogdan to turn and go in pursuit of the scumbag that had contributed to so much of the pain endured by the woman he now loved.

Books By Daniel Hurst

Have you read them all?

THE 20 MINUTES SERIES (in order)

20 MINUTES ON THE TUBE

20 MINUTES LATER

20 MINUTES IN THE PARK

20 MINUTES ON HOLIDAY

20 MINUTES BY THE THAMES

20 MINUTES AT HALLOWEEN

20 MINUTES AROUND THE BONFIRE

20 MINUTES BEFORE CHRISTMAS

THE INFLUENCING TRILOGY (in order)

INFLUENCE

INFLUENCER

INFLUENCED

STANDALONE PSYCHOLOGICAL THRILLERS

TIL DEATH DO US PART

Did you enjoy this book?

Reviews really are the most powerful way of getting attention for my books as honest reviews help bring in new readers.

If you have enjoyed this book I would be extremely grateful if you could spend a couple of minutes leaving a review on Amazon (it can be as short as you like).

Thank you.

About The Author

Daniel Hurst is the author of the 20 Minute Series, the Influencing Trilogy, and the bestselling psychological thriller, Til Death Do Us Part.

His online home is www.danielhurstbooks.com

You can connect with Daniel on Facebook at www.facebook.com/danielhurstbooks or on Instagram at @danielhurstbooks

He is always happy to receive emails from readers at daniel@danielhurstbooks.com